Also by Alex Morgan

THE KICKS SERIES

SAVING THE TEAM

SABOTAGE SEASON

WIN OR LOSE

HAT TRICK

SHAKEN UP

SETTLE THE SCORE

UNDER PRESSURE

IN THE ZONE

CHOOSING SIDES

BREAKAWAY

ALEX MORGAN

Simon & Schuster Books for Young Readers
New York   London   Toronto   Sydney   New Delhi

SIMON & SCHUSTER BOOKS FOR YOUNG READERS

An imprint of Simon & Schuster Children's Publishing Division

1230 Avenue of the Americas, New York, New York 10020

This book is a work of fiction. Any references to historical events, real people, or real places are used fictitiously. Other names, characters, places, and events are products of the author's imagination, and any resemblance to actual events or places or persons, living or dead, is entirely coincidental.

Text copyright © 2019 by Full Fathom Five and Alex Morgan

Cover illustrations copyright © 2019 by Paula Franco

All rights reserved, including the right of reproduction in whole or in part in any form.

SIMON & SCHUSTER BOOKS FOR YOUNG READERS

is a trademark of Simon & Schuster, Inc.

For information about special discounts for bulk purchases, please contact Simon & Schuster Special Sales at 1-866-506-1949 or business@simonandschuster.com.

The Simon & Schuster Speakers Bureau can bring authors to your live event. For more information or to book an event, contact the Simon & Schuster Speakers Bureau at 1-866-248-3049 or visit our website at www.simonspeakers.com.

Also available in a Simon & Schuster Books for Young Readers hardcover edition

Book design by Krista Vossen

The text for this book was set in Berling.

Manufactured in the United States of America

0222 OFF

First Simon & Schuster Books for Young Readers paperback edition June 2020

2 4 6 8 10 9 7 5 3

The Library of Congress has cataloged the hardcover edition as follows:

Names: Morgan, Alex (Alexandra Patricia), 1989- author.

Title: Switching goals / Alex Morgan.

Description: First edition. | New York : Simon & Schuster Books for Young Readers, [2019] | Series: The Kicks | Summary: Devin is spotted by an agent who wants her to model athletic wear, and soon she is juggling photo shoots, soccer games and practice, family time, and other activities.

Identifiers: LCCN 2018059667| ISBN 9781534427952 (hardback) | ISBN 9781534427969 (pbk) | ISBN 9781534427976 (ebook)

Subjects: | CYAC: Models (Persons)—Fiction. | Soccer—Fiction. | Friendship—Fiction. | Middle schools—Fiction. | Schools—Fiction. | Family life—Fiction. | BISAC: JUVENILE FICTION / Sports & Recreation / Soccer. | JUVENILE FICTION / Social Issues / Friendship. | JUVENILE FICTION / Girls & Women.

Classification: LCC PZ7.M818 Sw 2019 | DDC [Fic]—dc23

LC record available at https://lccn.loc.gov/2018059667

SWITCHING GOALS

CHAPTER ONE

"Devin, coming your way!" Jessi had just intercepted a pass from the other team, and two Panthers defenders were hot on her tail. I was closest, but I was hemmed in by Panthers too. She was desperately looking around the field to see who was open, but no one was.

At her words, I managed to slip by and free myself to receive Jessi's pass.

As soon as I got the ball, though, the defenders swarmed me. I searched the field, frantic for a Kicks teammate to pass the ball to. This had been a tough game. The Kicks were down five players because Grace, my co-captain, and some of the other eighth-grade players had been suspended. The score was 0–0, and we were in the last quarter. We had fought hard to protect our goal, but scoring chances had been slim.

If we got this score, we could win the game!

I eyed Frida. She usually plays defense but was pressed into playing midfield because we were missing players. She was open and in striking distance of the goal.

Our eyes locked, and I could see Frida's widening with fear. Frida is a fantastic defensive player. She defends our goal from strikers as if she were a leprechaun protecting her pot of gold. However, Frida was out of her comfort zone. Scoring opportunities were not in her bag of tricks. But I knew she had it in her. She just had to act like an offensive player!

Frida's skill on the soccer field comes from her acting talent. She recently had a starring role in the TV movie *Mall Mania* and was also in a bunch of commercials. Pretty cool, huh? Now each game we play, Frida pretends to be a different character. The Kicks have had on the field everyone from an Amazon warrior to a fairy princess to an army general. It sounds crazy, but it works. Frida's acting has given the Kicks an advantage in many games. And maybe it could now!

"You got this, Frida!" I said as I passed the ball to her, just as a Panthers defender tried to kick it away from me.

I watched as Frida expertly caught the pass, dribbled the ball closer to the goal, and then feigned a kick to the right. A second later she had planted the ball solidly in the back left corner of the net, while the goalie jumped for empty air to the right.

1–0! I looked at the clock. We only had nine seconds left in the game. Frida had just sunk the only goal in the game, which would give the Kicks the victory over the Panthers!

The crowd cheered when the ref called time. I saw Grace, Megan, Anjali, Jade, and Gabriela, the eighth-grade players who had been suspended for this game, on their feet and applauding for us. A rivalry with another team had almost gone too far, and Grace and her friends had planned to spray-paint Kicks-blue flowers on the field of the opposing team, the Roses, to send a message. I had tried to talk them out of it, but they were caught on the field by the Roses' coach right before they could paint the flowers.

They all regretted what had happened and were really disappointed in themselves that they had let the rest of the Kicks down by being suspended. They would have felt even guiltier if we had lost, but luckily we didn't, thanks to Frida!

Hands slapping me on the back in congratulations brought my attention back to the field and my teammates.

"Glad you got the ball to Frida, Devin." Jessi grinned. Her springy curls bounced as she landed next to me, still filled with energy from the game.

"It was thanks to you. That was a great steal," I said to my friend, and her smile grew bigger.

"You know, I'm starting to think we're a really great team," Jessi said, and I laughed.

"Yeah, I'm beginning to get that feeling myself." I grinned back.

"Devin!" Frida bounded over, her brown eyes widening dramatically as she stopped in front of me, placing a hand on her heart. "My first goal ever, and it's all thanks to you! I pledge my loyalty to you, from this day forth."

Um, did I mention Frida can be a bit dramatic? I guess it comes with the territory when you are an actor. When I lived in Connecticut, I didn't know anybody who was a TV star. It was just one of the many ways life was different in Southern California, like not having snow in the winter and always living under a drought warning.

"You don't need to do that," I told her. "You've always been an awesome defender. Now you just showed us you have the chops to score, too."

Frida shook her head from side to side. "No, it goes way beyond that. It's you, Devin. You've been good luck to me ever since we first met. Remember how I was terrible at soccer and didn't want to play?"

"How could I forget? You just sat on the field reciting Shakespeare. You didn't even try," I reminded her.

"Well, you were the one who helped me combine my passion for acting with my love of soccer," Frida said. "But I've been thinking. It goes way beyond that."

"Goes way beyond what?" Emma, the Kicks goalie, said. She jogged up to us with Zoe, a midfielder. They're some of the best friends I've made since I moved to California, along with Jessi and Frida.

Emma, one of the tallest girls on the team, stood about a foot taller than Zoe. Her long black hair was pulled into a ponytail, while Zoe's short strawberry blond bob was held back with a blue headband.

"I have finally come to realize that Devin was sent here, from Connecticut, to bring me good luck in all my endeavors," Frida stated.

Jessi shot me a look that was half eye roll, half surprise. "Huh?" she asked Frida.

"I think that Devin brought all of us luck when she moved here," Zoe jumped in. "The Kicks were the last-place team in the league, but thanks to Devin, we made it to the championships."

Frida sighed, her hand still on her heart. "It goes way beyond the soccer field, dear Zoe."

I could tell that both Zoe and Emma were trying to stifle giggles. Frida was really on a roll now.

"You see," she continued, not realizing her friends were holding back laughter, "when I got the callback for my second audition for *Mall Mania*, who was there? Devin! When I passed that science test—the one my mom said if I got a bad grade on, I would not be able to go on any more auditions—who was sitting next to me in class? Devin!"

I shrugged. "Yeah, I do sit next to you in science class. What does that have to do with anything?"

But Frida ignored me and kept right on with her monologue. "And when I had the pizza commercial audition, who told me to wear red, which turned out to be Chef Antonia's favorite color, which got me the job? You did, Devin!"

I vaguely remembered sitting in Frida's bedroom, with her frantically holding up different tops, and pointing at one and saying, "That one." But I didn't think that made me good luck.

"Yeah, I guess," I said, at a total loss for words.

Frida spread her arms wide open. "The bottom line is this, Devin. You are my good luck charm."

"Devin Burke, a human rabbit's foot!" Jessi joked, causing Emma and Zoe to crack up. "Do you come in pocket size?"

Since Frida was all wound up, she ignored Jessi's jokes and kept going as she pointed both her arms at me. "So you must, must come with me to my next commercial audition. It's this Tuesday after school. You cannot say no. I need you there. If you are, I know I'll get that part!"

I thought it over. I didn't know if I believed in good luck charms, but we didn't have practice this Tuesday, and I had never been to something like a commercial audition before. It sounded fun.

"If it helps you, of course I'll come," I told her. "I just have to ask my mom first."

Frida whipped her head around, looking at the soccer stands. "Mrs. Burke, yoo-hoo, it's me, Frida!" she called out before racing toward my mom, who was standing there with my dad and little sister, Maisie. They were all wearing Kicks-blue T-shirts to show their support.

"Okay, Lucky Charms," Jessi said as we watched Frida in an earnest conversation with my mom. "I'm going to start booking time with you. I have a killer algebra test on Monday."

"Ooh, can I have a lock of your hair? If I carry it around in my pocket, maybe it will bring me luck too?" Emma teased.

I threw my hands up in the air. "Come on, you all know what it's like when Frida gets an idea in her head. The best thing to do is just go along until she tires herself out."

"I think you're the one who is going to need the good luck," Zoe joked.

I wasn't worried. How bad could tagging along on one commercial audition be, anyway? It wasn't like anyone was going to be paying attention to me or anything.

CHAPTER TWO

"So what's the commercial for?" I asked Frida in between mouthfuls of pizza. Zoe, Emma, Frida, and I were hanging out at Jessi's house after the game. She has this really nice screened-in back patio, so we could enjoy the breeze without fighting the bugs for our pizza. Besides, Jessi claims that her new bedroom is too small to fit all of us. She's an only child, but that's about to change. Her mom is pregnant and expecting Jessi's baby brother or sister soon, so she had to give up her bedroom for the nursery.

"It's a totally fun new app," Frida said as she pulled her phone from the messenger bag that was slung across her shoulder. "It's called Flash Fortune, and it predicts your future. It works like this."

Frida held her phone up so we could all see it. A spinning disk filled with bright colors appeared on the screen, and then it stopped.

CHOOSE A COLOR flashed above it, and Frida tapped on the red portion of the disk. It started spinning again, and Frida was given the choice to pick another color. She did this five more times, and then the disk stopped, grew larger, and flashed the colors Frida had chosen in sequence, slowly at first, then faster and faster. As it did this, it said, "Fortune being calculated."

"I'm getting dizzy," Emma said, her eyes wide as she stared at the flashing lights on Frida's phone.

"It's almost done," Frida promised. With that, the lights stopped and the screen went dark before filling with stars. A button popped up that said, Click here for your fortune.

Frida clicked, and she read out loud what it said.

"'A great success awaits you.'" Frida squealed. "The commercial—I'm gonna get it! But I knew I would because Devin is coming with me to the audition. Here you go, Devin." Frida handed me her phone. "Give it a try."

I started choosing colors like Frida had done.

"Of course Devin would pick Kicks blue first!" Jessi chuckled.

"Now she's picking white and black!" Emma shrieked. "Soccer ball colors!"

I laughed. "You guys already told me that my brain is really a soccer ball, so why are you surprised?"

I waited as my fortune was calculated, then read it out loud.

"'Soon you will take a trip to a faraway place.'" I shook my head. "I don't think so. My grandparents were just here for a visit. My parents said we'd go back to Connecticut to visit them, but not until next summer."

"Hey! Maybe you'll be going to the next Women's World Cup. It's in France." Jessi gasped. "I'll go with you!"

"That would be awesome, but that's not exactly soon," I replied.

Frida shrugged. "You never know, Devin. The stars move in mysterious ways."

Uh-oh. Would this be Frida's next obsession? I could just see her walking around with a crystal ball and giant hoop earrings like a fortune-teller, predicting all of our next moves.

"Your turn, Zoe!" Frida grabbed the phone from my hand and passed it to Zoe, who took it reluctantly.

"I don't believe in this kind of stuff," Zoe said.

"It's just for fun," Jessi said. "Come on, Zo."

"Fine." Zoe gave an eye roll as she started her color selection and waited for the results. "'You will make a new friend,'" Zoe read from the screen.

"See!" Frida said. "That's a great fortune to get."

"Come on." Zoe sighed. "That could apply to anybody. It's not very specific."

"But it's something nice that *could* happen," Emma said. "Why not think the best? Now I want a turn!"

Emma took the app very seriously. "Oh, should I choose purple or pink? Maybe I'll choose pink first and purple second. But that could change my future!"

"Just go with your gut," Frida told her. "Don't over-think it."

But Emma still took the longest out of everyone picking her colors. Finally, after what seemed like an hour, she got her fortune.

"'You will learn to see things in a new way.'" Emma looked up with a disappointed frown on her face. "That's not much of a fortune. And I put so much time into picking the perfect colors too."

"What were you hoping to hear?" Zoe asked her.

Emma's cheeks turned red. "Maybe something about the cute new boy in our history class."

"Aha!" Jessi said triumphantly. "I knew you were crushing on him."

Emma blushed even further. "No, I don't even know him! He does look a lot like Brady McCoy, though." Brady McCoy was a pop star, and Emma was his number one fan. "I was kind of hoping the fortune would say I would at least talk to him or something, to find out what he's like."

"You don't need a fortune to do that," Zoe told her. "Just go over and say hi to him one day."

"Look who's talking," Emma shot back. "You are, like, one of the shyest people I know. You should get that it is not that easy to just start up a conversation with some random boy you don't know."

"Uh-oh, looks like making that new friend is going to be hard to pull off," Jessi teased Zoe.

"I guess I'm stuck with you guys." Zoe grinned at us.

"Looks that way." I grinned back.

"Gimme, gimme!" Jessi grabbed the phone from Zoe's

hand. "I'm next, and I can't wait to hear that I'm going to be a member of the US Women's National Soccer team one day."

Jessi chose her colors quickly and impatiently tapped her foot while the results were being calculated.

"'Your life will soon be in chaos.' Oh, great," Jessi moaned. "Why didn't I get a good one? Let me try again."

"Nope!" Frida grabbed her phone from Jessi's hand. "You'll confuse the cosmos. One fortune per day at most. You're better off doing it weekly, or even monthly."

Jessi arched an eyebrow, showing her disbelief. "Really? There's a science to this?"

"It goes far beyond science," Frida pronounced dramatically.

"Anyway, how's your mom doing?" Emma asked Jessi, changing the subject before Frida could get going.

"She's tired all the time. She's lying down now," Jessi said. Her dad had given us all a ride home from the game and had ordered the pizza for us to share. Usually when we go to Jessi's house, her mom, Mrs. Dukes, makes yummy and healthy snacks and lunches for us. But I wasn't complaining. Jessi lived near the Brick Oven, and they had some of the best pizza in the area.

"So, are you ready for your new baby brother or sister?" I asked.

"Ready as I'll ever be," Jessi said. "I helped Emma babysit her cousins last week to get more practice, and that helped."

"She even changed a diaper all by herself." Emma slung an arm around Jessi's shoulder. "I was so proud."

"Well, it was only a number one," Jessi said. "I'm not planning on doing those stinky number twos, that's for sure."

"Do you think it will be a boy or girl?" Zoe asked her.

"My dad thinks girl, and my mom thinks boy," Jessi said. "All I know is that it will be a baby, and either way it will be crying and screaming, so what does it matter?"

Frida said, "Maybe that's what the chaos is going to be!"

"Well, I knew that already!" Jessi laughed. "I didn't need the Flash Fortune app to tell me that."

"She's got a point, Frida," I agreed.

I knew Frida was taking the app, and all this good luck stuff, very seriously, but I didn't have much belief in it. I wasn't going to be taking a trip far away soon. But I guess it was all just for fun. Right?

CHAPTER THREE

The next day before dinner, I sat down at my desk in my bedroom to video chat with Kara, my best friend from Connecticut. There is a three-hour time difference between California and Connecticut. Sometimes I forget that and text Kara at nine at night in Cali, when it is actually midnight in Connecticut. Or sometimes Kara will want to talk to me, and it's five a.m. in California—a little too early for me. But overall we've been pretty good at figuring out the time difference and keeping in touch.

"Hey, Devin!" Kara's face popped up on my computer. She had her light brown hair pulled up on the top of her head in a bun. Wispy pieces fell from the bun and framed her face. It looked really pretty.

"Oh, I love your hair!" I said. "I'm going to try that."

"Hey, you've got that rocking beach hair going on, complete with highlights," she said. "Don't steal my look!"

I laughed as I touched my own hair. Playing soccer out in the Cali sun had added some blondish streaks to my brown hair, and when I take a shower at night, I always pull my wet hair into a messy bun. When I wake up in the morning and take my hair out, it's in nice beachy waves. That's my beauty routine—fast and easy. I usually prefer spending time on the soccer field, not in front of a mirror.

"Hey, I've got great news!" Kara's blue eyes got big and sparkly. "I was invited to Charlotte's sweet sixteen party!"

"Oh, wow! I'm so jelly!" I told her. Charlotte is a few years older than us. Her middle school soccer team mentored our elementary school team. Charlotte was one of the nicest girls I'd ever met, and besides being really cool and an awesome soccer player, she had taught me so much. Thanks to Charlotte, I became a better player. I'll never forget what she taught us about dribbling. While passing is important and shows good teamwork, Charlotte had explained, the best players in the world dribble the ball like it is part of their foot, without even looking down. She would hang around after practice and help us perfect this skill.

"You need a light touch," Charlotte had encouraged us as Kara and I practiced dribbling with both feet, seeing how many touches we could take between two cones set about two yards apart. "Some people prefer dribbling with the inside of their foot, others on their laces. Experiment and see what feels right for you."

Thanks to Charlotte, Kara and I both became really

good at dribbling, although it's a skill that takes years of practice to perfect. That feeling of the ball being an extension of my foot really helped me find my groove as a soccer player. I'll always be grateful to her for that. One of the reasons I liked helping out Maisie's elementary soccer team was because I wanted to pay forward what Charlotte did for us.

I suddenly realized how much I missed her. We've kept in touch on social media since I moved, but it hasn't been the same. I was happy for Kara but totally jealous I wouldn't be there to share the fun and excitement of Charlotte's big day.

"Don't be jelly, Devin. You're invited too!" Charlotte's face suddenly popped up on the screen.

"Charlotte?" I gasped.

"Surprise!" Kara smiled.

Looking at Charlotte's kind brown eyes and light red hair brought a rush of memories. She had taken us under her wing right away when her teammates started coaching us. Kara and I called her the Little Mermaid because of her hair, and she had thought that was funny.

"I know it won't be easy for you to come, since you live in California," Charlotte said. "But I wanted you to know that you're invited and I would love for you to be there. You're going to get an invitation in the mail, too."

"You've got to come, Devin!" Kara pleaded. "It will be so much fun to have you there, and I haven't seen you in forever!"

I was touched that Charlotte and Kara had planned out asking me during this call. It was such a great surprise! But I couldn't imagine any way that I'd be able to fly all the way out to Connecticut for the party.

"I absolutely want to be there," I told them. "Let me talk to my parents and see what they say."

Kara held up her right hand with her middle and index fingers intertwined. "Fingers crossed!"

We talked some more and caught up before I signed off. Then I hurried downstairs to catch my parents alone before dinner so I wouldn't have to have the conversation in front of my little sister, Maisie. She has a way of making everything about her!

The delicious smell of turkey bacon frying greeted me as I walked into the kitchen. My dad was standing over a pan on the stove, tending to the sizzling slices. My mom was at the counter, slicing up a loaf of multigrain bread she had bought at the farmers market that morning.

"Smells delish!" I said. "What's on the menu?"

My dad turned and smiled. "Turkey club sandwiches with avocado, and sweet potato fries," he said. "You've got perfect timing. The table is ready to be set."

"Sure," I said as I grabbed plates out of the cabinet. "Where's Maisie?"

"She earned twenty minutes of video game time," my mom said as she popped the sliced bread into the toaster oven. "She's got about five more minutes left."

Perfect! I thought. With my sister out of the way I

could talk to my parents about Charlotte's sweet sixteen party.

"So," I began as I placed the plates on our kitchen table, "I just got done talking to Kara."

"Your usual Sunday call?" Mom asked. "How is she?"

"She's good," I said. "But she had a surprise for me. Charlotte was there, and I got to talk to her, too."

"Really? What a lovely girl." Mom beamed. "She was so terrific with you and Kara. How is she doing?"

"Great! In fact, she's turning sixteen in a few weeks," I told Mom. I had to be careful at this point. Although I knew it would be a hard sell, I also knew from many years of dealing with my parents that phrasing things in the wrong way could get them shut down immediately, with no further discussion. So I had to tread carefully here.

I laid napkins next to the plates, carefully smoothing each one out and trying to act as casual as possible. "In fact, she's having this big sweet sixteen party in about a month. That's the reason she was on the call with Kara, to invite me. But I told her it would be impossible."

I pretended to be looking down at the table as I arranged silverware on top of the napkins, but I snuck a look at them with my eyes lowered.

They exchanged glances, and my mom pursed her lips together, then blew out air in her version of a sigh. She always does that when she is thinking something over.

"Hmmm . . . ," she said. "I don't know, Devin. Neither your father or I can take time off of work anytime soon, and I'm not sure if I'm comfortable having you fly out to Connecticut on your own."

My dad slid the turkey bacon out of the pan and onto paper towels on the counter. "And there's the cost. A plane ticket across the country isn't cheap, especially when you don't buy in advance."

I thought of Kara, Charlotte, and all my old friends in Connecticut getting dressed up and going to the party together, and it made me really homesick for the first time in a while. I love living in Cali, but this was really making me miss my friends back East.

Dad noticed my crestfallen face and came over to me, then patted my shoulder. "We'll talk more about it, Devin. But if you can't make it this time, we do have plans to go back East—all of us as a family—this summer. You can see Kara and Charlotte then."

But Charlotte's sweet sixteen was happening soon, not this summer! I wanted to shout. Instead, I nodded my head as I finished setting the table. I thought of the fortune I got when we played the Flash Fortune game yesterday at Jessi's house: *Soon you will take a trip to a faraway place.* I didn't know about everybody else's fortunes, but mine was definitely wrong!

CHAPTER FOUR

On Tuesday, Frida's mom picked us up from school to go to her audition.

"Nice to see you, Devin," said Mrs. Rivera as I slipped into the backseat. Frida climbed in next to her mom. "It's very nice of you to come along with Frida today. These things can take a while sometimes."

I shrugged. "I don't mind. I'm kind of curious to see what happens at an audition. Will there be any celebrities there? I've only seen one since we came to California, that time that Brady McCoy came to our fund-raiser. Maisie runs into them all the time. She saw Taylor Swift at a taco stand once, and now she acts like they're best friends!"

"I know," Frida said, and then she did a perfect impression of my little sister's voice. "'Taylor and I both got chicken tacos with extra salsa. Can you believe it?'"

"The funny thing is, my mom is pretty sure that it

wasn't even Taylor Swift. But you can't tell Maisie that," I said. "Anyway, I need another celebrity sighting so she'll stop talking about it."

Mrs. Rivera laughed. "I'm afraid that auditions aren't very glamorous. Usually Frida is just reading lines to a casting director or a producer. Especially for something small, like a commercial."

"A commercial is *not* small, Mother," Frida objected. "And please do not say that inside the casting office or I will have to pretend I don't know you."

"You do that anyway," her mom countered. "So that's not much of a threat."

Frida turned to me in the backseat and rolled her eyes.

"Are you nervous?" I asked, changing the subject.

"Not today," Frida said. She looked back at her mom. "I know I am getting the part. Do you know why?"

"Because you will be the most talented and qualified actor for the part?" her mom replied.

"Yes, but also no," Frida said. "Because besides my obvious talent, Devin is with me, and she is my good luck charm!"

I still wasn't so sure about that, but I didn't want Frida to lose confidence before the audition, so I kept quiet.

"And also, the Flash Fortune app told me," Frida went on. "'A great success awaits you.' That's what it said. Right, Devin?"

I nodded. "Right." Then I thought of my own fortune, the one I knew was wrong, and I kept quiet again.

"Frida, don't put too much faith in good luck charms," Mrs. Rivera told her. "Even when they're as nice as Devin, you have to have faith in yourself."

"I do, Mom," Frida said. "You know I do. But I am not going to ignore the signs all around me when the universe is shoving them in my face."

Mrs. Rivera sighed. "Shouldn't you be studying your pages?"

"I've got them memorized," Frida replied. "It's only two lines. But they're, like, the most important lines in the commercial." Then she frowned. "Although, maybe I should run through my expressions. I'm supposed to look confused, surprised, and excited. I'm pretty sure I've got confused and surprised down, but I think I need to work on excited."

She demonstrated by making this really wide, open-mouthed smile and raising her eyebrows so high, they disappeared under her bangs. She definitely looked excited, but kind of in the way a cartoon character would.

"Not bad," I said. "But maybe not so . . . extra?"

Frida nodded. "I knew it! I'll practice in the mirror. You don't mind, do you, Devin?"

I shook my head. "No, go ahead."

Frida pulled down the visor and started making faces in the tiny mirror. I scrolled through my phone. Charlotte was posting ideas for her party on Pinterest. It looked like she was doing a World Cup theme, with each table named after a different country, and cupcakes decorated like soccer balls.

Wow, she's still really serious about soccer, I realized. Then I had a pang of regret. Now it was going to be tougher than ever to miss that party!

As I scrolled through the pictures, Frida's mom pulled into the parking lot of a one-story stucco building with a line of palm trees out front.

"Here we go," Frida said. "Stick close to me, Devin."

"You got it!" I said. I hooked my arm in hers.

We entered the building into a narrow hallway lined with folding chairs that led to a closed door at the end of the hall. Already, there were a dozen girls and their moms and dads sitting in the chairs. A woman with short, white-blond hair and silver glasses was walking around with a tablet, and she approached us as we took our seats.

"Name," she said, in a flat voice.

"Frida Rivera," Frida replied, and the woman tapped the tablet screen. Then she looked at me.

"Oh, I'm not here to audition," I told her. She just stared at me, which made me nervous. "That's okay, right? I mean, it's okay if I hang out?"

The woman didn't even answer me. She just moved on to the next person.

"Well, she wasn't very friendly," I muttered to Frida.

"It's not an easy business," she replied. "You need to have a tough core to do it, like I do."

We sat down. "It's pretty competitive, I guess?" I asked.

Frida nodded, then motioned to a girl across the hall

from us a little ways down. She had wavy hair, the same auburn color as Frida's.

"That's Luna Murillo," Frida whispered. "She goes to a lot of the same auditions as I do. When I got the *Mall Mania* movie and she didn't, she moved to New York for two months to study acting with this top teacher there."

"Wow," I said.

"Yeah," Frida continued. "And then she landed the guest role on *Middle School Witches* that I lost last month. But I am so not worried about this commercial. Because she might have had fancy acting lessons, but I have *you*."

"I have nothing to do with it," I told her. "Your mom's right. It's all about you and your talent. You can do this!"

Frida shook her head but took a deep breath. "I've got this."

After that, we waited for a pretty long time while the other girls went into the room behind the door, one by one. When Luna went in, Frida didn't take her eyes off the door for one second. She came out after five minutes and stopped as she passed Frida.

"Don't even bother going in there," she said. "I nailed it."

"Yeah, well . . . that's what you say!" Frida replied.

Luna walked off, and I gave Frida a puzzled looked. "'That's what you say'?"

"I know, I should have had a better comeback," Frida said. "But that girl makes me so nervous! I bet she *did* do great. Maybe there *is* no point in me going in there. Maybe I should—"

"Frida Rivera." The blond woman called Frida's name.

"You can do this, Frida," I said. She still looked freaked out, though, so I figured I'd better go along with her superstitious stuff. "Your good luck charm is here. And the Flash Fortune app said you were going to get it."

"That's right!" Frida said. She jumped up. "I'm here!"

She marched into the audition office, followed by her mom.

"Just hang in the hallway, Devin," Mrs. Rivera said. "We'll be right out."

I nodded. There were still a few girls and their moms and dads left, but the hallway was empty. I stood up and stretched. I'd been sitting for way too long!

I steadied myself against the wall to do some calf stretches. Then I spotted a balled-up piece of paper on the floor and started kicking it around the empty part of the hallway. Eventually I kicked it through two legs of one of the folding chairs.

Goal! I congratulated myself.

"Devin!" I turned from my celebration to see Frida and her mom standing in front of the open doorway with another woman. Frida's eyes were shining with excitement.

"Thanks for coming, everyone, but you can all go home," the woman said, and the girls left in the hallway groaned with disappointment. I dribbled my paper soccer ball over to Frida.

"Does this mean you got it?" I asked.

"I did!" Frida squealed, and she hugged me. "You really

are my good luck charm, Devin!" I hugged her back. I still wasn't so sure about that, but I was excited for her anyway.

"Devin, are you in the business?" asked the woman who had dismissed the rest of the girls. She looked really professional in a black, sleeveless dress with no wrinkles, and her dark hair neatly pulled back.

"Me? No, I'm just Frida's friend," I said.

She handed me a business card. "I'm Ashanta Waters, and I'm a casting agent. I saw you playing around over there. I've been trying to find the right model for a shoot coming up, and I think you'd be perfect. I need someone tall and athletic to model workout clothing for girls."

"Um, thanks?" I said, taking the card from her.

"Ashanta is a wonderful agent," Mrs. Rivera said. "I can talk to your mom about it if you'd like."

"Think about it," Ashanta said, and then she ducked back into the room and closed the door.

"Devin, this is a-MAY-zing!" Frida said. "I booked the commercial, and you booked a modeling gig!"

"I don't know," I said as we walked outside. "I don't think I'd be a good model. I don't know anything about fashion. And I can barely take a decent selfie. I'm much more comfortable on the field with a soccer ball."

"Exactly! That's why she wants you—she needs an *athletic* girl. You're perfect!" Frida said.

"I'll think about it," I promised.

"Well, anyway, the Flash Fortune app was right!" Frida

said. "I am going to be such a great spokesperson for them now that I know it works. Maybe they'll send me on tour. I'd love to go to Paris. . . ."

While Frida kept daydreaming about her world tour, I looked at the business card in my hand.

Me, a model? I thought. *The app definitely didn't predict that!*

CHAPTER FIVE

"Devin! Over here!"

I kicked the ball to Grace, and she dribbled it down the field until she got into goal range. Then she kicked it over Zarine's head, and the ball bounced into the net. Score!

Coach Flores's whistle blared across the field. "Great scrimmage, everyone!"

We all jogged over to coach, panting and sweaty from the practice.

"Everybody, hydrate! Then I need to talk to you for a few minutes before I dismiss you," she said. She walked off toward the locker room while we got our water bottles.

"That sounds ominous," Emma whispered.

"Ominous. Wait, isn't that on our vocab list this week?" Jessi asked.

Emma grinned. "Ominous. Giving the impression that

something bad is about to happen," she recited. "I've been studying."

"Well, it *does* sound a little ominous," Zoe agreed. "Do you think there's more trouble over the whole blue roses thing?"

"I hope not," I said, taking a swig from my water bottle.

Frida took her phone out of her duffel bag. "Let's see," she said. She started tapping on her screen.

"Wait, are you checking the fortune app?" Jessi asked. "I thought you said you shouldn't check that all the time."

"Well, now that I've booked the commercial, I really need to use the app as much as possible so I can get into character," Frida replied. "Okay, here we go. It says, 'Don't worry. Be happy.' So Coach isn't going to say anything bad."

"I guess we'll find out," I said.

We headed over to the locker room and sat on the benches.

"I just want to begin by saying that I'm really proud of how you played on Saturday," she said. "Everyone had to step out of their comfort zone, and you did great."

Everyone started cheering and clapping.

"The suspension against some of our eighth graders has been lifted, and hopefully won't ever be repeated, so we'll be able to focus on our game against the Bayside Bolts this Saturday," Coach went on. "Keep focused and playing like you're playing, and we'll stay on track to make the playoffs."

We all cheered again.

"I've got one more thing to share. To make us stronger as a team, and to make sure we are following the highest principles of student athletes, I want to talk about doing community service together," Coach said. "I want the Kicks to be known not only for their skills on the field, but also their integrity off the field."

I saw the eighth graders who had been involved in the almost-spray-painting of the Roses' field shuffle uncomfortably and look at the ground. Coach Flores didn't have to spell it out. We all knew what she meant.

Coach continued, "I know in the winter league, Coach Darby had some of you visit a nursing home, and that was really successful. I've organized a time for us to walk dogs and clean cages at a local animal shelter. I've sent out an email to all your parents with the details. In the future, I'd love to hear any ideas you have about how we can help the community."

"I love helping animals!" Emma said.

Everybody began to talk about Coach's idea at once.

"I love dogs! They are soooo cute!"

"Sorry, I'm a cat person. I'll be with them."

"I'm not cleaning cages, but I will walk a dog."

"Great! I'll see everyone at Friday's practice!" Coach Flores called out over our voices, dismissing us.

Jessi's mom gave me a ride home from practice, and when I got there, I found Mom talking on her phone while Maisie did her homework.

"Thank you," Mom was saying. "I'll talk to Devin and then get back to you."

"Who was that?" I asked when she hung up.

"After talking to Frida's mom, I gave that agent a call," Mom said. Last night, I had spoken to her about Ashanta's offer and given her the card. Then, to be honest, I'd forgotten about it. The idea of me modeling seemed pretty out there.

"I should have mentioned when I gave you the card, I don't think that I'm interested," I told Mom. "But thanks for calling her."

"It's your decision," Mom said. "I'm not sure how I feel about you modeling, to be honest. It can be pretty stressful and competitive. But Ashanta's agency seems to be legitimate. And they certainly pay well."

That interested me. I hadn't really thought about getting paid.

"What did she say?" I asked.

"She said this job pays a hundred dollars an hour, and other jobs might pay more once you have some experience," Mom answered.

My jaw dropped.

Maisie looked up from her homework. "One hundred dollars! You'll be rich, Devin!"

"How many hours would I be working?" I asked.

"Four hours, minimum," Mom answered.

I started doing the math in my head. I could buy new soccer cleats with that money! Or . . .

"How much does a plane ticket cost to go to Connecticut?" I asked as Dad walked into the house.

"Who's going to Connecticut?" he asked.

"Nobody," I said. "I mean, if I take that modeling job, I could maybe make four hundred dollars, and I'm wondering if I could use that for a plane ticket to go to Charlotte's party."

"Or you could save it for something important, like college," Mom chimed in.

"Well Devin doesn't need to worry," Dad said. "She can get a soccer scholarship to college."

College? That's, like, five years away! I thought. *Should I be worrying about college already?*

I knew I had to play in college if I wanted to go pro. And I was pretty sure I wanted to go pro. Or play in the Olympics. But both of those goals felt like they were *way* in the future. I hadn't even been thinking about that.

"Devin, you could give some of that money to me, if you can't decide what to do with it," Maisie added. "Wait! I have a better idea! Why don't we ask the agent if they need a little sister for the modeling shoot?"

I rolled my eyes. "I'm not even sure if I'm going to do it, Maisie." I turned to Mom. "When's dinner?" I asked. I had to go think about all of this.

"In about a half hour," she replied. "We can talk more about Connecticut and what you want to do about this job opportunity later. Let's all get a chance to think it over."

I nodded and jogged upstairs. I took a quick shower and then called Kara on video chat.

"Hey, you're early," Kara said. "I just got home."

"Yeah, I wanted to ask you something," I asked. "Do you ever think about going pro?"

"Sometimes," Kara replied. "But mostly, I think I want to go to vet school. So maybe I'll play in college, but that's probably it."

I nodded. "You'd be a great vet," I said. "I don't have anything else that I care about as much as soccer. And it's always been my dream to go to the Olympics. So I might try to go pro. Is that crazy?"

Kara shook her head. "No, I totally think you could!" she answered. "You're an awesome soccer player. You sleep, eat, and breathe soccer. You should go for it."

"It seems like I have all the time in the world to figure it out, but I don't really," I said. Then I laughed. "Especially now that I could have a modeling career."

Kara's eyes got wide. "What?"

I explained to Kara about the modeling job. "It's ridiculous, right? I have no idea how to be a model. Just standing there and having someone pay you to take your picture? It sounds easy, but I don't know. . . ."

"Do it!" Kara urged. "Do it once, at least, and see if you like it. Why not?"

"What if I make a fool of myself? What if every picture is like this?" I pulled a silly face, with my eyes half closed and my mouth hanging open.

Kara laughed. "I doubt that will happen. Seriously, give it a try. If you hate it, you never have to do it again. But the Devin I know isn't scared of anything. You can try this!"

"Thanks," I said. "I've got to go eat dinner now."

Kara waved. "Bye-eeee!"

I closed my laptop and headed downstairs. Then I grabbed some plates from the closet and started setting the table.

"Mom, I think you should call that agent," I said. "I want to do the modeling job."

"Don't forget to ask about me!" Maisie said.

"Sorry, Maisie, but this is Devin's thing," Mom said. She looked at me. "I'll call her after dinner."

"Thanks," I said.

A little voice in my head began to scold me. *What are you doing? Do you really think you can model?*

Then another voice chimed in. *Do the job. Take the money. What can it hurt?*

Maybe I would hate it. Maybe I would love it. And maybe, just maybe, I'd make enough money for a trip to Connecticut, and my parents would let me go.

CHAPTER SIX

"Devin, hold still, please!" Mom said.

We were in my bedroom, and I was squirming as she tried to take my measurements with a long measuring tape. Everything had happened so fast. I had only decided yesterday to do this, and now I was having my measurements taken for a photo shoot that was happening tomorrow!

"I can't help it!" I said. "It tickles!"

"Well, we've got to get your numbers to the agency tonight so they have the right clothes for you tomorrow," Mom said. She sat down on my bed with a sigh. "Honestly, I didn't think this through when I said it would be okay for you to model. You're too young to be in an industry that puts so much emphasis on size and beauty."

"But this shoot is about sportswear, right?" I asked. "Isn't that a positive thing? I'm helping to promote physical activity."

"I guess," Mom said. "But I'm also not crazy about you missing school. *And* practice."

"I know," I said. "I really don't like missing practice. But I never do. And this is, like, a once-in-a-lifetime thing, right? I'll try something new, I'll make some money, and that's it."

I had some pretty good arguments for Mom because at lunch that day, I'd started to feel nervous about the shoot and missing practice, and Frida and Jessi had convinced me to do it. But that was before I'd known that my body would have to be measured. What if they didn't have anything that fit me?

"Well, we've already made a commitment," Mom said. "So we'll see it through. Now please just let me get your waist, and we're done."

As Mom wrapped the measuring tape around my middle, I had a thought.

"Nobody at the shoot is going to try to measure me, are they?" I asked, thinking it would be really uncomfortable to have a stranger doing this. "That would be weird. And what if my measurements aren't right? Will they send me home?"

"That's why we're doing this now," Mom said. "Besides, I'll be there the whole time if anything comes up. Maisie is going to go to Mindy's house after school. Dad will pick up takeout, and we can eat when we get home."

"Wow, thanks," I said.

"I'll pick you up at school at one o'clock," Mom said.

"And please, remember to wear a bra tomorrow. You'll need it for the shoot."

I felt my face flush. I'd just started wearing one last summer, and I hated it. Sometimes I avoided it if I could, except I always wore a sports bra for practices and games. But I suddenly realized that wearing one to the modeling shoot was probably a good idea.

"I won't forget," I promised.

Between the measuring and the bra, I was more than a little nervous when we pulled up to the photography studio the next afternoon. The large, high-ceilinged room had a big green wall right in the middle, and a guy was setting up props and stuff in front of it. Another woman was adjusting one of the tall, bright lights aimed at the wall.

Ashanta walked up to me and my mom.

"Devin, Jennifer, good to see you!" she said. "Jennifer, you can hang out over there." She pointed to some chairs facing the whole setup. "I'm going to get Devin into wardrobe and makeup."

Mom looked at me. "Do you want me to go with you?"

I kind of did, but I didn't want to admit it. "No, I'm okay," I said.

Ashanta led me to a room behind the green screen. On the way, a girl about my age, a little bit taller than me, walked past, and Ashanta stopped.

"Devin, meet Sabine. You two will be working together today," Ashanta said.

"Hey, Devin," Sabine said with a smile. She was dressed

in a pair of pink shorts and a white tank top with a matching pink stripe across the shoulders. She wore her curly black hair pulled back from her face in a ponytail, and her face looked like she was born for modeling, with smooth brown skin without a pimple in sight and long eyelashes.

I suddenly felt self-conscious. I'd never given much thought about how I looked. I liked the way the sun streaked my brown hair with gold. But of course there were things I didn't love. I always wore sunscreen, so my skin stayed pretty pale and never got tan, like some people's did. And I didn't have acne, but my cheeks sometimes got blotchy. I knew my friends wouldn't judge me, so I never worried before, but these photos would be seen by tons of people. Now all that stuff felt like it mattered.

Why did they ask me to model? Are they crazy? I thought. *Next to Sabine, I look like a modeling school dropout or something.* My palms started to sweat.

"See you out there," Sabine said, and I nodded silently and followed Ashanta, wiping my hands on my jeans.

We entered a room filled with racks of clothes and a table with a makeup mirror, a bunch of hairstyling stuff, and a makeup case that looked like the tackle box my dad uses when he goes fishing. But instead of fake worms, hooks, and lures, it was filled with makeup brushes, eyeshadow, and lipstick. A purple-haired young woman in cutoff jean shorts, vintage basketball sneakers, and a T-shirt with a rock band logo on it was looking through the clothes on the rack.

"Devin, this is Tenshi," Ashanta said. "She's going to

get you ready for the shoot. I'm going to leave you to it."

"Hi," I said shyly as Ashanta hurried off.

Tenshi nodded to me. "Sabine's in green, so I'm thinking blue for you," she said. Then she laughed. "Hey, I rhymed!"

"Yeah, you did," I said, but I let out a nervous breath instead of a laugh.

"I heard it's your first shoot," Tenshi said, and I nodded. "Don't worry. Zane, the photographer, is really chill. And Sabine's a pro. Just follow her lead."

I nodded silently again. Things were starting to feel overwhelming. I thought about bolting into the parking lot—I knew that Mom would follow me—but then Tenshi pulled out shorts and a cute shirt for me that were the exact shade of Kicks blue.

Frida would say this was a sign, I thought. So I didn't bolt. In fact, I thought of Frida and how she would act if she were here. She'd be totally confident. If Frida could channel Amazon warriors and fairy princesses on the soccer field, maybe I could channel Frida on the set today! I took a deep breath. I'd give it a try.

"Sit," Tenshi instructed, and I sat in a chair at the makeup table, trying to tap into Frida's self-assured energy. I had worn my lucky pink headband that I wore to all my soccer games to the shoot to give me an extra boost of security. Tenshi pulled it out before she sprayed some stuff into my hair then brushed it.

"Gotta tame those fly-aways," Tenshi said. "You should really use conditioner."

"I do," I said. "I use that two-in-one stuff."

Tenshi rolled her eyes. "That doesn't count!"

It didn't feel like we were off to a great start, and any trace of Frida slid right out of me, along with my lucky pink headband. Tenshi pulled my hair into a long ponytail that wasn't much different than my usual look, just less messy, and then she put some makeup on me. It felt like she was putting on a ton of stuff, but when I looked in the mirror after, it didn't seem like I had a bunch of makeup on at all.

"Awesome, right?" Tenshi said.

I stared at myself. I wasn't sure what she did, exactly. But my lips looked smooth and shiny. My eyes looked brighter. And my skin looked absolutely perfect. Not blotchy at all. But I still looked like me.

"Wow," I said.

Tenshi grinned. "You look great, Devin. Now get changed. There are some sneakers in there for you too."

I quickly got changed behind the privacy screen. The sneakers were Nikes, white with a blue swoosh. I slipped them on and looked in the mirror. I had to admit that it was a pretty cute workout outfit, something I'd actually wear, so that made me feel even better about taking the job selling it.

When I came out from behind the screen, Tenshi took me back out to the studio area. There was a guy with wavy brown hair carrying a camera, and he smiled when he saw me.

"You must be Devin," he said, coming over. "I'm Zane. Ashanta tells me you're a soccer player."

I nodded. "That's right."

"Great!" he said. "We're going to try some soccer-themed active shots today. The clothing company wants to get in on World Cup fever with their campaign. So maybe you and Sabine can do some soccer moves."

"Sure," I said.

Sabine walked up to us, smiling. "I've never played soccer before, so you'll have to show me the ropes, Devin."

Sabine's friendliness made me instantly more relaxed. I had remembered how mean Luna was toward Frida. I guess that, without even realizing it, I had expected Sabine to treat me the same way. What a relief that she was being nice!

I smiled back. "Okay." I couldn't imagine teaching Sabine anything about modeling, but soccer, I could do.

"Let's get some solo shots first," Zane said. "Sabine, I'll start with you. Can you do some warm-up stretches, maybe?"

"How about a yoga stretch?" Sabine asked.

"Sounds good," Zane replied.

Sabine got in front of the green screen and did some leg lunges with her arms straight up over her head. Zane put the camera on a tripod and began taking pictures. Then he started shouting out commands.

"Keep that neck straight!"

"Try it from the opposite side now."

"Okay, now look at the camera while you're doing it."

He was very nice about it, but really fast. And Sabine responded immediately every time he asked her to do something, moving into perfect position.

"Great!" Zane said after what seemed like a hundred different poses. "All right, Devin, how about some soccer stretches?"

"Sure," I replied, and I realized my palms were sweating again, but I didn't want to wipe them on my fresh blue shorts. I quickly blew on them and then stepped in front of the green screen. *What would Frida do?* I asked myself. She'd get right into the role of a soccer player. I knew how to do that in my sleep! So I confidently got on the floor and stretched out my left leg, pulling up the toes of my left sneaker, like I would before any soccer practice.

Zane took the camera off the tripod and crouched down. "Okay, nice. Hold that," he said. "Now try it with your right hand."

I pulled my left leg in and started to extend my right leg. Zane pulled the camera away from his face. "No, I mean, just use your right hand to pull back the foot on your left leg."

"Oh!" I said. "I mean, that's not how you do the stretch, actually," I said, but then I stopped myself. I could feel my face getting red. This wasn't about stretching. Was Zane going to be mad?

"Oh, sure, I get that, but let's just see how it looks with your hand crossing your body," Zane said.

I nodded and did the stretch the way he asked.

"Okay, now, eyes on your left foot," he said. "And smile."

I smiled, a full teeth-out grin.

"Try it with your mouth closed," he said. I did, but it felt sort of weird. "Okay, good. Now, that's more like a grimace. Just relax, Devin. Release your shoulders."

Release my shoulders? I wasn't sure what he meant, so I kind of just let them slump.

"Hmm," Zane said. "Can you do a stretch standing up?"

I jumped to my feet and pulled my right calf behind me with my right foot.

"Okay, that's interesting," Zane said. "Just do some more stretches. Don't worry about smiling. Pretend you're warming up for a game."

I tried to do that, but it wasn't easy with five people watching me. I did some shoulder stretches and then got on one knee to do some hip flexor stretches.

"Good!" Zane said. "Keep your back nice and straight, Devin. Now tilt your right shoulder toward me so I can see the logo on your shirt. That's it. Great!"

I glanced over at my mom, who was leaning forward in her seat and watching the whole shoot intently. She had a very serious expression on her face, and I couldn't tell if she thought I was doing a good job or a bad job.

"Try to smile again, Devin," Zane coached me. "Mouth closed. Great."

He looked up from the camera. "Okay, Sabine, get in there with Devin, please. And let's bring in the soccer ball."

One of the assistants came up and put a soccer ball at my feet. Sabine stood next to me.

"Maybe you could pretend like you're dribbling it, Devin," Zane said. "And Sabine could be on the other team blocking you or something."

"Sure," I said, "But shouldn't we be wearing soccer cleats?"

Zane looked over at Tenshi. "I don't know. Should they?"

Tenshi shrugged. "I don't know anything about soccer."

Ashanta spoke up. "This isn't a real game, Devin. The scene is just you and a friend kicking around a ball in a park. Does that work?"

I nodded. "Sure."

"Um, can you show me how I should be blocking you, Devin?" Sabine asked.

I had to think for a minute. "Well, I could pretend I'm about to kick the ball, and you could come in from over there, like you're going to intercept it," I said, pointing to a spot a few feet away.

"I can do that," Sabine said.

We got into position. I extended my right foot so it was almost touching the ball.

"Should I smile?" I asked.

"Let's try one where you're both looking determined," Zane said. "And Sabine, why don't you put your hands out in front of you, like you're blocking Devin?"

Oh boy, I thought. *Nobody in this room knows anything*

about soccer! But after bringing up the stretch, and the cleats, I wasn't sure if I should say anything else.

I decided I had to, though. This would be a pretty silly picture if I didn't.

"Um, Zane?" I began. "Nobody can put their hands on the ball in soccer except for the goalie."

"Well, Sabine can be the goalie, then," Zane said, and he was starting to sound a little bit annoyed.

I decided not to push it. Zane took some shots of Sabine blocking me with her arms, and then we did some where it looked like I was chasing her, and one where I was passing the ball to her. I really did pass it on the last one, and it rolled right past her and bounced into the wall. I almost forgot that I was at a shoot instead of on the field. That felt the best to me. It got me out of my head and stopped me from worrying if I was grimacing or whatever Zane had said I was doing. Who knew smiling could be so hard? After that, we took a short break for some water.

"You're doing great, Devin," Sabine told me.

"Thanks, but I'm not so sure," I said. "You're, like, an expert at this."

Sabine laughed. "I've been doing it since I was three," she said. "Probably as long as you've been playing soccer, right?"

"Right," I said, and that got me thinking. Me jumping into modeling might be just as crazy as Sabine joining a soccer game without ever playing before. What had I been thinking?

"What do you think? Do you like it?" Sabine asked.

"It's cool," I said. "But I feel like I'm not doing anything the way Zane wants me to. And the whole shoot is kind of confusing. I mean, what's the point of having a green background behind us, no matter what we're doing?"

"That's called a green screen," Sabine explained. "Zane can go into the photo and digitally add any background to it, like a park or a soccer field or something like that."

"Wow, I had no idea," I said. "Is there a green screen at every photo shoot?"

Sabine shook her head. "No. I've shot in all kinds of places. In restaurants, the aquarium, the beach . . ."

I was learning so many new things. "So basically a model is kind of an actress, too," I said to Sabine. "You have to act like you can play soccer, or are at a beach or a restaurant."

"Yep, that sums it up!" Sabine said. "As you can tell, I don't know the first thing about soccer. I'm glad you do. If there is someone on set who actually knows how to do whatever it is we're pretending to do, it helps."

"Zane didn't seem too happy with my feedback," I reminded Sabine.

She laughed. "It's true, they are all about getting the best shot, which might not always align with reality. Remember, they are taking hundreds of photos. You need to relax and have fun with it. You're bound to get some good shots in there, even if some don't feel right."

Then Zane called us back to continue the shoot, and

we did a bunch of other more static shots. Sabine holding the soccer ball. Me sitting on a bench, lacing my shoes, while Sabine propped one foot on the edge of the bench like she was talking to me. Then we changed into leggings and tank tops and did it all again. I remembered Sabine's advice, that they were taking a ton of shots of every pose. So I just tried to go with it and have faith that there were some great shots in the bunch.

"Okay, that's a wrap!" Zane called out. "Thank you, girls. You did a great job."

I changed back into my own clothes, and when I checked my cell phone, I was surprised to see it was after six o'clock.

"Wow, that went fast," I told Mom as we left the building.

Mom yawned. "Not for me. That was a long afternoon."

Sabine waved to us from her mom's car. "Bye, Devin! Hope we get to work together again!"

"Bye!" I called back.

"So, what do you think, Devin?" Mom asked. "Would you want to do it again?"

I had to think about that. "I'm not sure," I said. "It was interesting, seeing how it all worked, and it was fun getting to know Sabine. But I don't think they'd want me to do it again. I couldn't figure out how to smile! And I don't think Zane liked it when I kept correcting him about the soccer stuff."

"Devin, you have the most beautiful smile in the whole world!" Mom said.

"Of course you think that. You're my mom," I said. Then I gave her one of the closed-mouth smiles Zane had asked me to do. "It's goofy, right?" I asked. "I mean, I feel goofy when I'm doing it."

Mom laughed. "Okay, maybe *that* smile is a little silly," she agreed. "But I think you did great, Devin. I really do. I saw some of your photos on the screen. They looked really great."

"Uh-huh," I said, and I looked at my goofy smile in the mirror. I wasn't so sure.

It's a good thing I don't want to be a professional model! I thought. *At least, now I can concentrate on soccer again!*

CHAPTER SEVEN

"Devin, concentrate!"

Jessi's voice snapped me out of my head and back into the warm-up for the Kicks game against the Bolts. Coach Flores had us taking turns in two pairs. Jessi and I were one pair, and Frida and Anna were another. Jessi and I were the attackers. We had to keep possession of the ball for thirty seconds while Frida and Anna attempted to steal it from us.

Anna had swooped in and stolen the ball from me after barely ten seconds, passing it to Frida. Coach Flores blew her whistle, and the four of us left the center of the field.

"Great, now do two laps around the field," Coach Flores told us as Zoe, Grace, Anjali, and Sarah took our places in the warm-up exercise.

"What's up, Devin?" Jessi asked as she jogged next to me. "You're usually laser-focused on the soccer field. But you definitely weren't paying attention back there."

I sighed loudly. "I just got all in my head about playing against the Bolts today. They're one of the best teams in the league."

Jessi nodded. "That's what I've heard. But they've never played the Kicks before."

"Yeah, but getting into the playoffs in the fall means we're playing some different teams this time around—better ones," I said. I bit my lip. "It probably wasn't a great idea for me to miss practice yesterday."

Jessi and I were running side by side as we talked. We were right around the same height, so it was easy for us to keep pace with each other.

"Aw, come on, Devin." Jessi shook her head, her springy curls bouncing in the high ponytail she had pulled them into for game day. "You are the Kicks' best player. Missing one practice isn't going to change that. Your soccer-ball brain is just getting the best of you!"

I chuckled. "Yeah, I guess so. When Anna stole the ball from me, I was thinking of something Jamie had told me." Jamie and I were on the same winter league team, the Griffons. We started out not liking each other much but ended up as friends. "She said the Bolts were hard to beat, and really fast."

"Oh yeah? Let's see them catch me!" Jessi started sprinting ahead of me.

Jessi zoomed around the field. "Save it for the game!" I called to her just as Coach Flores's whistle blew.

"Come on, everybody, grab a drink before the game!" Coach Flores said. "And then you can do your sock swap!"

The sock swap was a pregame Kicks tradition that we started last fall. After grabbing some water, we all flopped down together in a circle on the grass before each of us took off one sock (Coach Flores let us wear socks with any pattern we wanted) and passed it to the teammate on our right. By the time we hit the field, none of the Kicks were wearing matching socks. It was funky and fun, and I loved it!

I took off one of my socks. They were bright Kicks blue, like the outfit from the shoot, and had pink pigs with balloons tied around their middles floating in between white, fluffy clouds. Ever since we started doing the sock swap, my mom's been on the hunt for fun socks for me, and she especially liked this pair.

"Get it? When pigs fly?" she had chuckled when she gave them to me.

"Wait, is that a comment on our ability to win?" I had asked.

Mom had gasped. "Oh no! I didn't mean it that way at all! Should I take them back?"

"I'm kidding. They're cute," I had told her.

For this sock swap, Emma was sitting next to me, so I handed her my sock.

"I love it! Oink, oink!" Emma snorted, then laughed.

Jessi was sitting on my other side. She gave me one of

her socks, a bright pink one dotted with black-and-white raccoons dressed up like ninjas.

"The Bolts won't be able to catch our ninja raccoon feet," Jessi joked. "They'll never see our kicks coming." She leaped to her feet and got into a karate stance, moving her arms and hands slowly in the air.

"Oh!" Frida exclaimed, coming to stand next to her. "I needed a role for this game. I could get into being a ninja. What's my character's motivation?"

Zoe frowned in concentration, her forehead wrinkling. "How about the soccer ball contains the stolen jewels of a royal ninja family. Anyone who keeps them from falling into enemy hands will not only be a hero but will also win the hand of the prince in marriage."

Frida wrinkled her nose. "Marriage? No thanks! I'll settle for my reward in riches and fame."

Zoe shrugged. "Fine by me. Most fairy tales have some guy winning the hand of the princess. I thought we could turn the tables."

Frida nodded thoughtfully. "A modern interpretation of a classic. I like it! But what—what does he look like?"

Zoe laughed. "That's totally up to you."

"Okay, girls!" Coach Flores said. "You've got this. Just go out there and do your best, like I know you can. Zarine, you're starting on goal. Let's see Sarah, Anjali, Jade, and Frida on defense. Jessi, Taylor, Maya—you're my midfield. Devin, Hailey, Grace—I want you on forward."

I nodded, excited to be starting the game. I looked up

into the stands. Since we were playing on the Bolts field, there were more Bolts fans than Kicks fans. But I knew I had my own fans cheering us on, and that's when I spotted my mom, my dad, and Maisie sitting in the bleachers. I waved, and they waved back.

"Okay, soccer-ball brain," I whispered quietly to myself. "Focus on the field, not self-doubt, and we've got this."

The game started, and I could see from the get-go that Jamie was right. The Bolts zipped around the field like lightning and were great at stealing. However, fast didn't always equal accurate. Many times the stolen balls went shooting out-of-bounds a few seconds later. When that happened, the Kicks were able to take possession and throw the ball back into the game. Remembering advice that Coach Flores had drilled into us gave me the confidence to handle the throw-ins like a pro.

"Now remember"—I flashed back to a practice with Coach Flores—"every throw-in is a game-changing opportunity, but you have to think it through. Remember, you can turn throw-ins into goals. If you get the ball into your hands, then panic and throw the ball blindly, it won't be helpful. Stop and think: What do you need to do? A long throw can help attack and advance on the goal. A short throw can help you gain ground. You've got to think fast while you've got the ball in your hands. It takes practice to perfect it."

And practice we had, with a ton of different throw-in drills. Throw-ins happen at every game, but those practices were especially coming in handy against the Bolts!

At one point, I had driven the ball down the field and was in scoring range of the Bolts goal, when one of their defenders came upon me suddenly with that lightning speed and kicked the ball out from under me. The kick had no aim, and the defender wasn't passing it to anyone. All she was trying to do was get the ball away from me. It worked, but the ball went shooting out-of-bounds.

I raced over to throw the ball back into the game. Grace had carved out some space for herself within striking distance of the goal, and I knew a long throw-in to her could result in a scoring opportunity for the Kicks.

Just like we had practiced about a million times with Coach Flores, I grasped the ball firmly between both hands, my fingers making a W shape as I held the ball in front of me. I took a big step forward as I moved the ball up and behind my head, getting ready to throw it. Using the force of my entire body, I powered the ball toward Grace, who expertly caught it with her feet and drove it into the goal. We had scored!

"Yes! Perfect long throw-in, Devin!" Coach Flores cheered from the sidelines, and I raced over to Grace to slap her on the back.

"Great catch." I grinned.

"Great throw." She smiled back.

But there wasn't time for chatting. We had to hustle. The game started up again, and the Bolts were getting aggressive and running us ragged with their speed. The Kicks were trailing by one goal when the second half of the game started. We had possession of the ball a lot but kept getting stuck in midfield and unable to make any progress toward the Bolts' goal. Then, with just a few minutes left in the game, the Bolts stole the ball and kicked it out-of-bounds again.

I had another opportunity for a throw-in. Once again I assessed the situation. A long throw wouldn't work this far up the field. My best bet was a short throw-in to Jessi, who could move it down the field toward Grace.

I tossed the ball high to Jessi, setting her up for a header. She leaped up to meet the ball, bouncing it off her head toward Grace, but a Bolts defender swooped in at the last moment and kicked the ball away from Grace.

"Darn it!" I muttered under my breath, frustrated. The Bolts were turning out to be every bit as good as their reputation.

As time on the clock was running down, I knew we had to tie it up to force a shoot-out; otherwise, we would lose.

After getting possession of the ball back, the Kicks managed to move the ball closer to the Bolts' goal. I was trying to create space and keep my distance from those dangerous Bolts defenders when we got another throw-in chance. Taylor took this one and sent a long throw my way.

I felt the excitement rising. This was it! I could score and give us a chance at the win. I ran as fast as I could to outpace those speedy Bolts defenders while Taylor sent the ball flying in the air ahead of me. I had to dodge and weave without losing sight of the goal.

My foot connected and sent it flying into the goal, high above the goalie's head. I had done it! I tied up the score and forced a shoot-out. The Kicks had a chance at beating the Bolts!

I raced away to share the joy with my team when I heard the referee's whistle blowing repeatedly. "Offsides! Offsides!"

Who? Me? I thought. Ugh! I slapped my forehead with my palm. My heart sank as I realized what had happened.

While I was trying to run faster than the Bolts and get the ball that Taylor had thrown to me, I must have outrun the nearest Bolts defender, putting me closest to the goal before the ball hit the ground.

It's all right, I thought. *We'll get the ball back. I'll get another chance. . . .*

Tweeeeeet! The ref's whistle blew.

"Game over! The Bolts win!"

The stands erupted in cheers for the Bolts. I face-palmed.

"It's okay. Great game." Jessi came up to me, panting. "They were tough."

I sighed. "Yeah, but I should have been paying better attention to where I was."

Jessi dug her elbow into my ribs. "You are a world-famous supermodel now. You've got other things on your mind besides worrying about who is closer to the goal—you, the ball, or the nearest Bolts defender."

"Ha ha," I said sourly, not in the mood to be teased about it just yet. Was that really the reason I'd messed up our chance to tie the game?

"Come on." Jessi threw her arm around my shoulder. "Let's go shake hands with the other team. We've got to give them some mad respect—they were awesome."

"No prince's hand in marriage for me," Frida chirped as we lined up. "Oh well. I've still got my commercial."

Even though we had lost, the rest of the Kicks were in a good mood. We had played our best against a tough team and held our own.

"Don't beat yourself up, Devin." My dad knew what I was thinking as soon as I walked off the field toward my family. "That was a tough game, and you were mentally and physically drained by the end. Anyone could have made that same mistake. Focus on the good. Your throw-ins have really improved. I can see the wheels spinning in your brain as you check the field. It's a great skill to have."

"Thanks, Dad." I gave him a big, sweaty hug.

As we loaded into the Marshmallow (that's what we call our family's white minivan), my mom shared some news.

"During the game, Ashanta called," she told me as Maisie and I buckled up in the second row of the van. "She wanted me to tell you that the photos from the shoot came out terrific. She was really happy with them, but more importantly, the client was thrilled."

"Wow," I said, my mouth hanging open in surprise. "I didn't think I did such a great job."

"You did," Mom said. "In fact, you did such a great job that Ashanta wants to know if you want to do another shoot for a clothing catalog this week."

I frowned. "I don't know. . . . When is it?"

Mom smiled. "I know exactly what you are thinking. It's on Tuesday, when you don't have soccer practice."

That was a relief. I wasn't entirely sure about the whole modeling thing yet, and if it meant distracting myself and letting down my team, I didn't think I'd do it again. But if I didn't have to miss practice, maybe I'd give it another shot. If it could help me afford a ticket to Charlotte's party, it was worth it. My parents hadn't made a decision yet, but I might as well earn some extra money while I had the chance.

"Since I don't have to miss practice, I'll take the job!" I said. "After today's game, I need all the practices I can get."

I sighed as I settled back into my seat. Even if I blew the soccer game, at least I was winning at something!

CHAPTER EIGHT

The following Monday at school, I was sitting in the Kentville Middle School cafeteria with Jessi, Emma, Zoe, and Frida, eating lunch.

"They were as wild and unpredictable as lightning," Frida said about the Bolts as we rehashed Saturday's game. "They've definitely earned their name!"

"Just like the Kicks!" cheered Emma. Officially, our soccer team was the Kentville Kangaroos, but the team was nicknamed the Kicks years ago because of our great kicks!

"Except the Bolts zapped us," I said, frowning. "Especially when I made that boneheaded offsides move."

Jessi slammed her hands down on the cafeteria table.

"Ugh, Devin. Knock it off!" she growled. "You are way too hard on yourself. We all make mistakes sometimes. Nobody can be perfect, on the soccer field or off."

Emma just laughed. "Yeah, remember when I scored a goal for the other team? Or when my cleat shot off my foot and I became an Internet meme? You can't even compare one offsides in a game to that!"

I frowned again, but this time for a different reason. Was I making the game all about me? As I've been told ever since I started playing soccer preschool, there is no "I" in team.

"You know what? You're right," I admitted. "We all make mistakes sometimes. We're a team. I shouldn't be focusing on one mistake, even if it was mine. What we should be focusing on is ways to counteract the Bolts' speed and aggressiveness the next time we play them."

Zoe sighed. "I'm a little soccered out. We've been talking about it ever since the game. What about our community service next Sunday at the animal shelter? Do you think we'll have to pick up dog poop?"

"Any way you look at it, my future is filled with poop," Jessi groaned. "Baby poop, dog poop . . . What's the difference?"

Frida shook her head. "Nice subject change. From soccer to poop. I haven't finished eating yet, people! But anyway, your future isn't filled with poop, Jessi. Remember? The Flash Fortune app said chaos was coming your way, not dog poop."

Jessi rolled her eyes. "I think I'd prefer the dog poop."

"I asked Coach Flores what we would be doing," Emma said. "She said the shelter would want us to play with and exercise both the dogs and cats. We can take the dogs for walks, and the cats have a room where they can roam free, and there are a bunch of toys you can use to interact with them."

"Unless you want to practice your new diaper-changing skills on some of the dogs." I couldn't resist teasing Jessi.

Jessi blew out a big mouthful of air in an exaggerated sigh. "This conversation makes me believe my life is already filled with chaos." She stood up. "I'm going to see what Sebastian and his crew are up to. I'd rather hear some sci-fi geek convo than another word about dog poop."

With that, she marched over to her friend Sebastian's table and stood there talking to him and his friends.

I shook my head and began piling my garbage from lunch onto my cafeteria tray. Usually my mom packs me something healthy, but today she gave me money to buy lunch, and I had splurged on some chicken fingers and french fries. Even though my mom reminded me there are healthy options available in our cafeteria, like salads and veggies, or today's special of whole wheat spaghetti with turkey meatballs, I decided I eat plenty of turkey meatballs at home, and I could not resist the smell of the fries.

I did take a picture of the fancy spaghetti and meatballs, though, and texted it to Kara. Our school cafeteria back in Connecticut never had anything like that on the menu.

I was walking over to the trash can to dump out my

stuff when I ran into my friend Steven, who was doing the same.

I am kind of crushing on Steven, and Jessi has been crushing on Steven's best friend, Cody. Recently things had gotten complicated, though, when Jessi started hanging out with Sebastian, who was a cute sci-fi geek, while Cody was a cute athlete.

According to our parents, Jessi and I aren't allowed to date boys, but we are allowed to hang out in groups with some of our guy friends. When I thought that Jessi and Cody weren't going to be friends anymore, I thought I wouldn't be able to see Steven as much. But Jessi and Cody worked it out. Jessi is friends with both Sebastian and Cody, and I've hung out in groups with both of them. So it all worked out, and I was relieved. I really liked spending time with Steven. He has a soccer-ball brain like I do!

"Hey, I heard the Bolts gave you a hard time on Saturday," Steven said. "If they are as fast as the boys' team, you must have been running like crazy to catch them."

"Oh, man." I slumped next to the trash can. "They were zipping around the field. Whenever we had the ball, they would kick it out-of-bounds."

Steven laughed. "I wonder if the boys' and girls' teams practice together. The boys play just like that too."

"Have you played them yet this spring?"

"Nope, but we did last fall. They had us running in circles," Steven said. "Hey, did you get a chance to study for the World Civ test today? I hate having tests on a Monday. Mr. Emmet is getting harder as the year goes on."

"I studied last night," I told him. "He said it was going to be multiple-choice, no essay questions, so it should be a breeze."

"Some of us don't breeze through our quizzes, Devin," Steven told me. "I studied a little bit on Saturday morning but not at all last night. Would you mind cramming with me? We've got about ten minutes left before lunch is over."

"Definitely," I said. "I really don't want to go back to our table and have another talk about poop."

"Poop?" Steven asked as he arched his eyebrow. "You Kicks really have some interesting lunch conversations."

I laughed. "You don't know the half of it. Let me get my backpack—I'll meet you in a sec."

As I grabbed my backpack from our table, I heard a murmur in the cafeteria and the sound of rushing wheels.

I looked up, and I saw Arlo, an eighth grader, zooming past me on a skateboard, holding a cafeteria tray loaded high with a plate of spaghetti and meatballs.

"Arlo, Arlo, Arlo, Arlo!" I heard voices chanting from the table next to us. Arlo had been sitting there with a bunch of his eighth-grader friends, and they were laughing and pointing as they chanted his name. I grabbed my backpack and Zoe shook her head.

"They just dared Arlo to deliver lunch to Stella on his skateboard," Zoe said. "Apparently he's crushing on Stella."

Stella was also in eighth grade. "But if Assistant Principal Castillo sees him, he's in big trouble."

Skateboarding in or anywhere near the school was a big no-no. There were a bunch of kids, mostly eighth graders, who brought their boards in and left them in their lockers, taking them out at the end of the day to use at the skate park a couple blocks from the school. Because of this, students could have skateboards in their lockers but were never ever allowed to use them on school grounds. Arlo was going to get himself in big trouble.

I watched as Arlo skateboarded from one end of the cafeteria to the other, tray in hand. As he got close to Sebastian's table, where Jessi was standing, a girl suddenly pushed her chair out to get up. She didn't see Arlo coming toward her!

Arlo tried to steer his skateboard around her, but he was going too fast. The skateboard skidded, and Arlo began to lose his balance.

He tried to steady himself, but the tray in his hands flew up in the air. A hush fell over the cafeteria as everyone watched the plate of spaghetti and meatballs soar up into the sky in what seemed like slow motion.

"I've got it!" Arlo yelled as he reached for the plate. As he caught it, though, he tripped over his skateboard, and the plate flew up into the air again, this time landing upside down on the nearest person's head. And that person just happened to be Jessi!

"Arrrrggggggghhhhhhh!" Jessi yelled. The paper plate

looked like a silly white hat. Red sauce dripped down her face, and spaghetti noodles hung over her head like a weird wig.

As everyone watched, astounded, the plate slid off Jessi's head and down her body, leaving a trail of sauce, bits of spaghetti, and meatballs down her whole outfit.

"Jessi!" I cried, and I ran over to her.

Then Mrs. Castillo's voice rang out through the cafeteria. "Arlo Anderson! My office, immediately!" Arlo put his head down and skulked out of the cafeteria while everyone laughed.

"This is not funny!" the assistant principal barked. She shook her head. "We've been lenient letting students keep skateboards in their lockers. If this is how you are going to behave, then that privilege is revoked until further notice. Just being seen with a skateboard on school grounds will result in immediate detention. Understood?"

The cafeteria grew quiet as she walked over to Jessi. Mrs. Castillo shook her head. "Oh, Jessi, how awful! I'm going to make sure you get an apology from Arlo. We are going to have to call your parents. You need to go home and take a shower. You are covered in sauce. I've never seen anything like this. What chaos!"

Jessi sighed. "Let me get my backpack."

All eyes were on her as she walked back to the table. I walked with her silently, not sure what to say. Part of me wanted to laugh, but I knew Jessi wouldn't find it funny right now.

Frida looked up at us, her eyes wide. "Chaos! Jessi's fortune has come true."

"Aw, come on, it's just a coincidence," Zoe insisted.

Frida smirked. "Let's see. Two fortunes down. Mine came true, and now Jessi's. I wonder who will be next: Emma, Zoe, or Devin?"

Zoe just shook her head. "No way. I don't believe in this stuff."

"How can you deny it?" Frida asked Zoe. "Look at everything that happened so far, including me getting the commercial and scoring the winning goal in our game against the Roses."

"If Devin and you have that whole lucky vibe thing going, then why didn't we win the game against the Bolts?" Zoe shot back.

Frida waved a hand in the air as if dismissing the idea. "Good luck doesn't mean everything is going to go your way every single time. In fact, we could have lost by a lot more to the Bolts. And it's not like we asked Flash Fortune about that game and it told us we were going to win."

Emma wasn't paying attention to the back-and-forth between Zoe and Frida. Instead, she was looking freaked out.

"Maybe that spaghetti was meant for me!" she said. "Maybe I was supposed to get sauce in my eyes and see things in a new way, like the fortune-telling app said." She shuddered. "I'm scared. Since the spaghetti didn't get me, I could be in store for something worse!"

I didn't know if I believed in any of this. I mean, Frida *did* get the part she wanted, and Jessi definitely did get caught up in chaos. But both of those things could have been coincidences. I mean, Frida got the part because she's a good actress, right? And there's almost always chaos in our cafeteria.

A little part of me hoped Flash Fortune was real, though. It would be really cool if my fortune came true. Who knew? If I did a really great job at the next modeling shoot, I could earn more money and get to go to Charlotte's sweet sixteen party!

CHAPTER Nine

That night, I started to get a little nervous about my photo shoot the next day after school. I guess I had done a decent job, or Ashanta wouldn't have offered me another one. But I definitely hadn't been in my comfort zone the first time. The soccer field was where I felt confident. At the last shoot, I got to pretend to be playing soccer. That helped me feel more comfortable. If I didn't have that going for me at this shoot, would I be a complete disaster?

After I finished my homework, I started to think about soccer versus modeling. Why did I feel so much more comfortable on the soccer field? Maybe natural talent was part of it. But also, I practiced my butt off, so I was prepared. *Do models practice too?* I wondered.

At the photo shoot, I'd had trouble smiling naturally. Zane had even told me that I looked like I was grimacing.

So I decided I could practice smiling—although I had no idea how to do that!

I stood in front of the full-length mirror on the back of my bedroom door and gave a big smile. My eyes were wide and popping out of my head, and you could see every single tooth in my mouth. I didn't look happy at all.

I shook my head. No good. And I felt really silly. While I never felt silly playing soccer, sometimes I wanted to learn new techniques, and there were a lot of great tutorials online. Maybe there was the same for modeling?

So I opened my laptop and found a bunch of tutorials about how to smile like a model. I watched a ton of videos and then tried out the techniques. One of them was to close your eyes and take a few relaxing deep breaths before opening your eyes and smiling. The other was to relax your jaw and face muscles, which at first I did too much, and my face looked droopy. I also tried a technique that said to pretend someone you really liked was behind the camera, so I pictured Kara encouraging me, and that seemed to help.

I tried a closed-mouth smile, a partly-opened mouth smile, and smiling with my hands on my hips. Then I smiled while I tossed my hair over my shoulders and almost cracked myself up when I saw myself in the mirror.

I even practiced something called smizing, which is when you "smile with your eyes" instead of with your mouth. I widened my eyes, I wiggled my eyebrows, I narrowed my eyes, and I cracked up again. I still looked ridiculous!

But I didn't give up. I practiced smiling until my cheeks hurt. I flopped onto my bed, exhausted, while I massaged my face with my hands. Could you sprain your cheeks like you could sprain your ankle? Who knew modeling could be so dangerous!

Even though it felt super weird spending all that time looking at myself in the mirror while I practiced smiling, it definitely helped me feel less self-conscious. I really liked the idea of pretending Kara was taking the picture, and thinking of silly jokes we shared. That seemed to get my smile to be more natural. And practice had helped me relax my facial muscles, so I didn't feel all tense and weird when I smiled. I was totally feeling more confident.

Bring that feeling to the shoot with you tomorrow, I coached myself. *If you can, you'll be smiling like a pro!*

My mom picked me up after school the next day so we could drive right to the photo shoot.

On the way over, I video chatted on my phone with Kara.

"I can't believe that my bff is going to be a famous model!" Kara gushed. "I always thought you'd be a famous soccer player, Devin. But your life is so glamorous since you've moved to Cali. Meeting the pop star Brady McCoy, having a friend who is an actress—nothing like that ever happens here in Franklin."

Franklin is the Connecticut town my family lived in before moving to California. It's a really pretty town, with tree-lined streets and some old houses that date back to the 1700s. The leaves on the trees would turn orange, yellow, and red each autumn before falling off. I really missed that, and the change of seasons in general. We'd also get huge snowstorms in the winter, and snow days where we wouldn't have to go to school. Kara lived only a few blocks away from our old house, so I'd go to her house and we'd build snowmen or take our sleds up to the hill in her backyard and go racing down. Then we'd have hot chocolate and cinnamon toast and warm up in front of Kara's living room fireplace.

I felt a wave of homesickness overwhelm me, and my eyes filled up with tears.

"Devin, what's wrong?" Kara asked, her brow creasing with worry.

I was sitting in the passenger seat next to my mom, and I saw her shoot me a glance out of the corner of her eye. This is why I usually video chat with Kara in the privacy of my own bedroom, but I needed a pep talk from my very bestest friend before the photo shoot.

I decided to be honest, even with my mom listening.

"When you mentioned Franklin, I just got all homesick," I told Kara. "I'm so lucky that I've made so many great friends in California, but I miss you and our old house so much sometimes. I wish I could come back for Charlotte's birthday party to visit."

"Yeah, what's the status on that? Any chance you can come?"

With that, my mom jumped into the conversation.

"We are considering it, Kara." My mom raised her voice a bit so Kara would be able to hear her. "It's a little tricky because it will involve time off from school for Devin, the plane trip is expensive, and on top of that, Devin would be flying alone. It's a long flight."

"I did it, Mrs. Burke." Kara had come to California for a surprise visit last fall. "It wasn't so bad. I had a direct flight, so it wasn't like I had to change planes or do anything scary. Plus, the flight attendants knew I was traveling alone and were super nice, and someone from the airline escorted me from the plane to the gate where you and Mr. Burke picked me up."

My mom nodded slowly. "You know something, Kara? I had forgotten all about that. With the airline's help, it could be a possibility if we can work the rest out."

I opened my eyes and mouth wide as I gave Kara an excited smile over the video chat. I couldn't believe it! She gave me a thumbs-up and used the chat to type "One reason down, two to go!"

With that, my mom pulled into the parking lot of the photography studio, and I signed off with Kara. I didn't think it would be hard at all for me to smile now.

Mom had explained to me that even though Ashanta had gotten me the job, this one was for a different client, so it would be at a different place with different people. This photography studio was in a similar building, but instead of a green screen, there was a big white background for the photos, and instead of Zane, the photographer was a woman with a sleek ponytail. And while I had hoped that Sabine would also be doing the shoot, I didn't see her. Instead, there was a girl with curly hair who reminded me of Sabine with her flawless skin. I just hoped she was as nice as Sabine! When I walked in, she was laughing and talking to two boys about my age whom I guessed were also models.

The one familiar face was Ashanta, who greeted us when we came in. "Great, you're here! Let's get started. Jennifer, you can take a seat, and I'll get Devin into wardrobe and makeup."

"Okay, we know the drill now," my mom joked as she sat in one of the chairs at the far end of the room. She pulled a book out of her purse.

Clearly, my mom was a lot let less anxious this time around, and I found, to my surprise, that I was too. I knew what to expect now, I'd practiced, and even if I didn't do things perfectly, I'd give it my best. The game against the Bolts proved to me that mistakes happen. You just have to dust yourself off and move on. Plus, this time I wasn't missing school or practice.

Still, I was relieved to see Tenshi in the makeup room. She gave me a big smile when I walked in. Today, her purple hair was styled into a fauxhawk, and she had on big, black military boots that laced up to her knees. As intimidating as she looked, I was glad she was there.

"Devin, awesome!" she said. "It's always nice to see the same faces again."

I sat in the tall chair in front of me so she could work her magic.

"Ashanta probably already told you, but this is an activewear shoot for the Athlead website and catalog," she said. "I've got a couple of great looks for you. You are, like, a total natural in the fitness wear stuff."

"I should be," I told Tenshi as she tickled my eyelids with a makeup brush. "I spend most of my time in my soccer uniform or my workout clothes. And for school, I usually just wear shorts, a T-shirt, and flip-flops."

I guess I never really thought about it, but if I was being paid to wear fitness clothes for a modeling shoot, my soccer uniform—and even my shorts and T-shirts—would be considered fashion too!

As Tenshi finished my makeup and started working on my hair, I told her all about Zoe. "She's totally into all different kinds of clothes," I said. "She's always wearing the latest styles and mixing and matching patterns and colors. If I tried to do that, I'd look like a clown. But Zoe always looks like she stepped out of a magazine."

"Next time, you should bring her along with you," Tenshi said. "She'd probably love seeing behind the scenes, and it sounds like she has the makings of a great stylist."

"That would be fun!" I said as Tenshi pulled my hair into a long ponytail. I couldn't believe I hadn't thought of that before. Tenshi and Zoe would get along great!

"I'd love to try some other looks with your hair. It's so

pretty," Tenshi said wistfully. "But for activewear, ponytails are the go-to hairstyles."

I couldn't help but look at myself in the mirror after Tenshi had finished. I really liked the way she made me look. Tenshi made it seem so easy, but I wouldn't have known where to start. *It would be nice if she lived in our house; I could look like this every day for school*, I mused. I needed to pay more attention to how Tenshi did my makeup, although it was kind of hard because my eyes were closed most of the time. I wouldn't mind learning a few tricks. I don't know if it's something I'd want to do every day, but if the mood struck me, I wanted to be prepared.

I went behind the privacy screen to change into the workout outfit: long leggings in a tropical floral-print pattern with a matching sports bra. The sneakers were pink and gray, and not really a shoe I'd ever use to work out. They were more about fashion than function, and pretty flimsy, with not much arch support. But I reminded myself that this wasn't an athletic match, and I was selling the outfit, not the shoes.

When I walked back into the studio area, the girl who looked like Sabine nodded to me.

"Hey," she said. "I'm Crystal."

"Devin," I said.

She turned her back to me and starting talking again to the two boys I had seen earlier. I stood there, not sure what to do, and feeling kind of dismissed. Was Crystal going to be more like Frida's frenemy, Luna? I had hoped she'd be cool like Sabine.

Luckily, the boy who had long, curly blond hair pulled back into a messy bun, and reminded me of Arlo and the other eighth-grade skateboarders, introduced himself to me.

"I'm Troy, and this is Malik," he said.

Malik and I exchanged grins, while Crystal looked bored, staring at her fingernails.

"Did Tenshi give you that haircut?" I asked. "It's really cool. I like it."

Malik's dark hair was parted on the top and had lots of volume, but it was cropped close around the ears, so it had a fauxhawk look going on, like Tenshi's.

Malik laughed. "Nope. In fact, she saw my hairstyle, and that's when she started rocking her own fauxhawk."

Crystal pretended not to hear and instead started whispering to Troy. I ignored her, and Malik and I continued chatting until I felt someone grabbing my arm.

"Devin," my mom said urgently. "We have to talk. I don't want you photographed wearing only a bra."

I felt my cheeks turn red as my mom dragged me back to Tenshi's room. I avoided making eye contact with Crystal, Troy, and Malik, although out of the corner of my eye, I saw Crystal smiling at my discomfort. *Why do moms have to be so embarrassing?* I thought. *Couldn't she have said something to me when we were in private?*

"Mom," I whispered, "this is what I wear when I go for

a run in our neighborhood. And Crystal is dressed in the same thing." Crystal was wearing ombré leggings in sky blue with a matching sports bra.

"Crystal is not my daughter," my mom said. "And this is going to be online and printed in catalogs. It's not the same as going for a run in our neighborhood."

I wanted to point out that anyone could snap a picture of me anytime during my run and I wouldn't even notice. But I decided to keep my mouth shut, because than I might be forced to wear a tracksuit for my runs, the velvet kind, like my grandma wears.

"What's up?" Tenshi said as we came barreling in.

"I'm not comfortable with Devin being photographed in only a sports bra." My mom sounded tense, like she was expecting an argument.

Tenshi frowned. "I know the client needs shots of the sports bra for the catalog," she said. "Let me think. . . . I've got the matching windbreaker for that outfit. It's really cute. Would it be okay if Devin wore the windbreaker open on top?"

"Can I see it?" my mom asked.

Ugh, I wanted to crawl behind the racks of clothes, curl up, and die of embarrassment.

Tenshi put the windbreaker on me and tugged at it a few times, eyeing it critically.

"This will work," she said to my mom. "Are you okay with it?"

I held my breath as I waited for my mom's response.

She slowly nodded. "Yes, I think that is definitely more appropriate."

"Great!" Tenshi smiled. "Just so you know, the other looks are tanks and tees."

"Good!" My mom smiled in return, and then we went back out in the studio.

"Ooh, cute windbreaker," Crystal said, all smiles in front of Tenshi. I guess she wasn't going to snub me in front of the crew.

"I have one that matches your outfit too," Tenshi said. "But would you mind doing a few shots without it?"

Crystal shrugged. "Of course. I don't have a problem with it," she said while shooting me a superior, smug glance. I had met Crystal's type before on the soccer field, so it didn't throw me. However, since I was a lot more secure on the field than in front of the camera, I had to work extra hard to make sure that she didn't get under my skin and diminish the newly-gained confidence I had discovered during my practice session.

I was relieved that we had found a solution that made my mom happy, but it felt weird that only Crystal had to do the shoot in the bra. She didn't seem to mind, though, and I saw a woman who looked like her mom sitting on the side with my mom. Her mom was obviously okay with it.

It was all kinds of confusing, and my mind was racing as Jeannie, the photographer, began using Malik for a few test shots.

"We're ready to start," she said after a few minutes. "Malik and Troy, I want to get the two of you together first."

The boys posed together as if they were hanging out at the park after school. Then Jeannie had them do some very plain shots, with them standing with their backs straight and posing to show off the clothes.

They're naturals, I thought to myself, in awe. Before, I would have thought it was easy to just look like yourself, but now I knew now how much work it took to smile and look natural for a camera.

Crystal was standing next to me, watching the boys, and I thought I'd try one more time to break the ice. After all, some of my biggest rivals on the soccer field, like Jamie from the Rams, ended up becoming friends.

"They are good," I whispered to her.

"They've been doing this for years, like me," Crystal told me. "In fact, Malik is also an actor. He's been in a few commercials. Is this your first shoot?"

"It's my second," I said, but then it was our turn to be photographed.

First, the shots were straight posing, hands on hips, not doing any action. This was a little trickier for me because I was more comfortable moving. But my practice session in front of the mirror the night before had given me confidence and I was feeling at ease when the photographer asked me to smile and change positions.

The afternoon went fast because we had to keep changing clothes and posing. At the end, we all did a shot together, the four of us, and got to play around however we wanted, and that was when I felt in my element—in motion. Malik and Troy started tossing a football to each other, and I jumped up and intercepted it. Then I tossed it to Crystal, and she ran across the studio.

"Touchdown!" she yelled, and we all laughed. The actions shots were definitely my favorites.

"Settle down, everyone, please," Jeannie said. "I just need one more shot."

"What if we get in a huddle? We do it before every soccer game to get us all charged up."

Jeannie shrugged. "Let's give it a try. It can't be a real huddle—you'll have to all face the camera."

We got into a semicircle and placed our hands on top of one another's. The photographer liked it so much, she even had us turn our backs to the camera, with our arms around one another. Then she asked us to drop our arms and turn our faces to look at the camera over our shoulders.

We all started spontaneously high-fiving, and the photographer snapped photos like crazy. Then she had the idea for us to do a real close circle huddle, and she slid on her back along the floor and took photos of us while we looked down at the camera.

"Great idea, Devin! I love this. I'm getting great stuff!" Jeannie said.

I felt my confidence soar from her praise, and I started to truly have fun, posing for the camera and feeling more like I belonged.

Flash! Flash! Flash!

"That's a wrap!" Jeannie said. "Thanks, everybody."

I relaxed and headed into the makeup room to get changed. On my way out, Ashanta approached me.

"Nice job today, Devin," Ashanta said. "You've really loosened up in front of the camera. I'll definitely be getting more work for you."

I beamed. The whole session had been a lot more fun, even with my mom totally embarrassing me!

On the way home from the shoot, my mom pulled into a spot in our bank's parking lot.

"Can't you just go through the drive-through?" I complained. I was still a little upset with her.

"Oh, no, Devin," Mom said. "You are coming in with me to open a savings account. This is your first job, and I want you to learn how to save money for your future. You know your dad and I started a college savings account for you when you were born. It's up to you if you want to contribute to that from your earnings, but I wanted you to have control over this account and decide how to use it."

I thought about it for a second. "How about I put half of the money I earn into my college account, and the rest into the new one? That way I'll have some options."

My mom leaned over the seat and gave me a hug. "Have I told you lately what a smart young woman you are? That's a great idea. I'm very proud of you for saving for your future."

I hugged my mom back, forgetting all about the total

humiliation at the photo shoot. I was lucky to have a mom who looked out for me in every way possible. As for the future, I could try for a soccer scholarship, but if I changed my mind, I'd have some savings, too. It felt good not to have to make any big decisions right now AND to have some money in the bank. And I didn't need the Flash Fortune app to let me know that whatever the future held for me, I'd be ready!

CHAPTER TEN

"Heads up, Grace!" Emma called out during a scrimmage in soccer practice the next day.

Whomp! The next thing I knew, a soccer ball was bouncing off my head.

"Emma, what was that?" I asked as Jessi intercepted the ball and took it down the field.

"Sorry!" Emma called back. "I thought you were Grace!"

Weird, I thought, but I didn't have time to dwell on it. I shook it off and charged down the field, hoping to get the ball back. In the end, Jessi's team won the scrimmage.

When we finished, Coach Flores called us together for a talk.

"I see some of you running around out there at superspeed, like the Bolts," Coach said. "Don't be the Bolts. Be the Kicks. Speed is good, but it can lead to mistakes. The

Bolts went out-of-bounds so many times during the game that I lost count."

We all nodded.

"Saturday we're playing the Flying Bees from Harrison," she went on.

"Bees? Ouch!" Emma blurted out.

"It's another team we haven't faced before," Coach said. "Don't let that worry you. Just get out there and play your best on Saturday. Focus on what *you* can do, not on what they can do. Because what you can do is pretty great!"

"Go, Kicks!" Grace yelled, and we all started to cheer.

Jessi's mom gave me a ride home from practice, and when I walked into the kitchen, Dad was chopping up vegetables and Mom was slicing grilled chicken.

"Dinner salad?" I asked.

Mom nodded. "With lots of avocado, promise! Now why don't you go shower before dinner?"

"Sure," I said, and I took three steps toward the stairs and then stopped.

Maisie was standing in the kitchen doorway. She had her hair pulled into a messy bun, and she had makeup on her face. A *lot* of makeup. Dark streaks on her cheeks and down the bridge of her nose. Thick black eyeliner and purple eye shadow. She'd done something to her eyebrows, so they were dark brown, darker than her hair.

I was stunned. "Maisie—what?"

"I'm going to go with you on your next modeling

shoot," she said. "I'm going to be discovered, just like you."

Mom looked up from the cutting board. "Oh my goodness, Maisie. What have you done?"

"I found a makeup tutorial online," she answered. "Everybody is doing this look."

"Not everybody who is eight years old," Mom scolded. "Did you use my makeup for that?"

"Whose else would I use? Devin doesn't have any. And she's supposed to be a model." She shook her head, like *I* was the one who was acting ridiculous.

Dad was trying not to crack up. Mom just kept shaking her head.

I couldn't help myself. "Maisie, what kind of makeup look is that supposed to be? It's a little bit . . . extra."

"It's from Bethany Pierre, and she has two million followers," Maisie replied. She pointed to the dark lines on her cheeks. "This is called contouring." Then she pointed to her eyes. "Bethany says that purple is on trend right now. Only she calls it orchid."

"Maisie, go wash that off," Mom said.

"That's not fair!" Maisie cried. "Why does Devin get to be a model and I don't?"

"I'm not really a pro model, Maisie," I said. "I'm just trying it out."

"Then why can't I try it out?" Maisie asked.

Mom sighed. "Maisie, I'm not really sure how I feel about this whole modeling thing. It's already making you think you have to wear makeup, and I certainly don't want to expose you to any more of that at your age. Now please go and wash your face."

Maisie frowned, turned around, and stomped up the stairs.

Dad and I burst out laughing.

"That was . . . frightening," I said in a loud whisper.

"Poor Maisie," Dad said through his laughter.

"This isn't funny!" Mom said firmly. "Don't you see? Maisie felt like she needed to wear all that makeup to be 'discovered.'"

"Well, I don't even wear that much makeup at the shoots," I said. "She just doesn't know better."

"I know," Mom said, "but how do you feel during the shoots, Devin? Do you ever feel, like, uncomfortable? Like you're being judged for how you look?"

I had to think about that. I'd felt uncomfortable at first being poked and prodded, but no one had ever told me there was anything wrong with how I looked or tried to make me something I wasn't. I didn't feel like I needed to wear makeup, but I liked what Tenshi put on me when I was there.

"It's okay," I said. "I don't feel weird or anything. I kind of like it. And I still look like me."

"Well, that's good to hear," Mom said. "I just hope you would be honest with me if you ever felt differently. Promise?"

I nodded. "I promise," I said. "So what are you going to do about Maisie?"

"If she really wants to model, she can wait until she's twelve, like you," Mom said. "I think that's fair."

"It's not fair!" Maisie marched back in the room, her face scrubbed but with some traces of makeup still streaked on it.

"I'm sorry you feel that way, Maisie," Mom said. "Now can we please all have a nice dinner together? Devin, you can shower after; we're just about ready now."

Maisie frowned and didn't reply. She and I set the table, and Maisie was quiet as she poked at her salad. I usually don't feel bad for Maisie, but today I did. She had tried really hard with that makeup, even though it was a mess.

"Maisie, you can come to a shoot with me if I get another one," I offered. "See what it's like."

Maisie looked up from her plate. "Really?" she asked hopefully.

"That's very nice of you, Devin," Mom said. "Maisie, you are welcome to come, but I have to warn you, modeling shoots can be long and more boring than you think. You'll have to bring a book to keep you busy, like I do."

Maisie nodded. "Yes, yes, I will!" she said, smiling again. "Maybe I'll get discovered!"

"If you do, we'll have to tell them to wait a few years," Mom said.

Maisie considered this. Finally, she nodded. "Good. That will give us time to work out a fair contract." She turned to me and smiled. "Thanks, Devin."

Maisie doesn't smile at me a lot. Usually, she's just

being annoying. But I was starting to figure out that it might not be easy being a little sister. She got to see me doing all kinds of cool things that she wasn't old enough to do yet. When I was little, I'd never had that experience. I always got to discover new things on my own.

"No problem, Maisie," I told her.

Just as we were finishing diner, Mom's cell phone beeped, and she picked it up.

"Wow, that's weird," she said. "It's Ashanta. She wants to know if you can do a shoot on Saturday morning."

I frowned. "I don't know. I have a game at one o'clock. Would I be done on time?"

Mom quickly texted. "Ashanta says it's one look, in a park, and the call time is eight a.m. It should only take an hour or two. So you'd be done in time for the game."

I thought about it. I didn't like the idea of cutting it so close to my game, but a photo shoot in a park instead of a studio sounded like a lot of fun. And maybe if I made more money, I could keep working on the plane ticket idea with Mom.

"Do it, Devin!" Maisie urged. "Do it! Do it!"

"Okay, I'll do it!" I said.

"Yay!" Maisie cheered.

I'll get up extra early that day and go on a run, I thought. *I'll be ready for the game! Ashanta hasn't steered me wrong yet.*

The next morning at school, I noticed that Emma was missing from the classes that we had together. She wasn't in the cafeteria when I got there, either.

"Has anybody seen Emma?" I asked Frida, Zoe, and Jessi when I reached our lunch table.

"No," Zoe replied. "It's weird. I texted her to see if she was out sick, but she didn't reply. I'm worried that something might be . . . Oh, wow!"

Zoe's eyes had gotten big, and she was staring past me. I turned to see Emma there. She didn't look sick at all, but she *was* wearing glasses.

"Emma! Is this why you were out this morning?" Zoe asked.

Emma sat down next to Zoe and sighed. "Yes."

Zoe took the glasses off of Emma's face. "They're so cute! I love these frames. Turquoise tortoiseshell. Very cool."

"After school I'm going to practice putting in contacts," Emma said. "The eye doctor said they're easy to use and they'll be better when I'm playing soccer—"

"Wait, what exactly happened?" Jessi interrupted. "One day you didn't need glasses, and now you do?"

Emma shook her head. "Actually, I've been having trouble seeing things in the distance for a few months now."

"Like at practice yesterday, when you thought I was Grace?" I remembered.

"Exactly," Emma answered. "Mom noticed me squinting, so she made an appointment with the eye doctor for me. So here I am." She put the glasses back on and made a face.

"Don't do that! You look adorable!" Zoe told her.

Emma unpacked her lunch. "I guess," she said. "I'm just a little upset because it's so complicated, you know? Now I always have to remember glasses, contacts, eye exams. What a pain!"

"But this is good news for your soccer game," Jessi pointed out. "You were a great goalie before, and you couldn't see the field that well. Imagine how much better you'll be now that you can see clearly!"

Frida gasped and dropped her sandwich. "Emma, of course! It's your fortune! 'You will learn to see things in a new way.'"

"Whoa," Emma said, her eyes wide. "You are right!" She shivered. "Okay, this is starting to get creepy."

"Don't be silly," Zoe said. "My fortune hasn't come true. And neither has Devin's. And as for your glasses, there are lots of ways to 'see things in a new way.' It's just a coincidence!"

"Are you kidding? I got glasses! It's not a coincidence—it's real!" Emma said. She turned to Frida. "You need to ask the creators of their app how it works. Maybe they're real-life wizards or something."

"I think they're just two software guys from Oakland," Frida replied. "But I bet they would love to get a testimonial from you."

"Did you film the commercial yet?" I asked.

Frida nodded. "Yes, and I'm going back to do a photo shoot for a print ad," she said. "Hey, did you really do a second modeling gig? Is this a new career for you, Devin?"

I shrugged. "I don't know. I mean, I'm starting to like it. And I have another shoot on Saturday."

"We have a game on Saturday," Jessi reminded me.

"I know that," I answered. "The shoot is early. I'll make the game."

"You'd better!" Jessi said. "I know I said not to worry so much, but don't give up soccer just to take some pictures."

"Hey!" Frida protested.

"You know what I mean," Jessi said. "I mean, modeling is cool, I guess, but soccer is *important*. You know?"

"What's so much more important about kicking a ball up and down a field?" Frida shot back.

"Sports develop skills like cooperation and discipline," Jessi countered.

"You need those things to be a model, too," Frida said. "Right, Devin?"

Frida was right. I used to not realize it, but you definitely had to work together on a shoot. Not only was there teamwork involved, but you also needed to practice and be able to take direction. Modeling required a lot more skills than I had originally thought. It was more than just being able to take a pretty picture. Yet there was something more energizing about teamwork on the soccer field. I did feel more important as part of a soccer team than I did as part of a photo shoot, but maybe that was just because I had a soccer-ball brain. The experience had definitely given me a lot to think about.

"I like doing both," I said. "But I guess soccer will always come first. At least I think so."

"Then why are you doing modeling instead of the game?" Jessi asked.

"I never said that. I told you I'm doing both," I said. "It won't be a problem."

Jessi didn't look convinced. "Hmmm."

"Don't worry, Jessi," I said. "I won't let you down."

CHAPTER ELEVEN

By 11:55 on Saturday, I knew I was going to let Jessi down. And not just Jessi—my coach, my team, and myself.

Things had started going wrong the moment I woke up. I had forgotten to set my phone alarm, so I didn't get in the morning run I had planned. Instead, I woke up to Mom shaking me awake.

"Devin, we've got to get to that shoot by eight!" she said. "Hurry up and get dressed as quickly as you can."

I slowly opened my eyes and picked up the phone on the side of my bed. "It's only seven o'clock."

"And the shoot is forty-five minutes away," Mom said. "If there's traffic, we'll be late. So make it fast, Devin!"

I took a quick shower and left the house with my hair wet, dressed in the only clean clothes I could find in my drawers: a pink T-shirt with hearts on it and purple sweatpants. I slipped on flip-flops and went downstairs, where Maisie was anxiously waiting.

"Wow, Devin. You don't look like a model today," Maisie said. "Maybe they'll ask me to take your place."

That's when I noticed that Maisie looked pretty adorable, in a white sleeveless dress with little blue flowers on it. A matching flowered headband pulled her brown hair away from her face.

"Maybe they will," I said. I couldn't argue. I definitely didn't feel like a model at that moment.

I grabbed a protein bar and a yogurt shake to eat in the car, and we drove to the park, making it just in time. The whole scene looked chaotic. There was a trailer set up and a bunch of people walking around carrying phones and electronic equipment and stuff like that. I didn't see a familiar face this time.

A woman with a clipboard walked up to me.

"Devin? One of Ashanta's, right?"

I nodded. "Yes. Is she here?"

"Nope!" the woman said. "Okay, I need you in the wardrobe trailer. Thanks."

Mom and Maisie followed me to the trailer, but I went inside by myself. I was hoping to see Tenshi, but instead I found a woman with short black hair.

"Who are you?" she asked me in a flat voice.

"Devin Burke," I replied.

She looked me up and down. "Really? Okay. You're gonna need some extra time in the hair chair. Go see Gary."

She pointed to a guy with spiky blond hair standing behind a hairdresser's chair.

"Hi," I said. "I'm Devin."

"Have a seat, Devin," he said. He slid the ponytail holder out of my hair. "Oh boy. You know they make this thing called a hairbrush, right?"

I could feel my cheeks getting hot. "Sorry. I was kind of in a hurry this morning."

Gary started spraying stuff in my hair and sighed. "Don't worry, we'll fix this in no time!"

In ten minutes my hair was sleek, shiny, and bouncing on my shoulders. I'd never done a shoot with it down. Then the woman with dark hair, Delia, instructed me to change into some black leggings with a pink tank top and matching hoodie. In the changing area in the back of the trailer, I found three other girls getting dressed. Nobody said hello.

Okay, it's kind of like a locker room, I thought, and I quickly changed into the workout outfit. Then I headed outside. Mom and Maisie were sitting on a park bench—well, Mom was sitting, but Maisie was standing in front of her, doing model poses. Mom was shaking her head. I walked over to the other girls who had been in the changing room with me. Maybe it would be easier to talk to them when we weren't all getting dressed, I reasoned.

"Hi," I said. "I'm Devin."

They were all staring at their cell phone screens.

"Aubrey," said a girl with freckled skin and straight blond hair, looking up for one millisecond to nod at me.

The brown-skinned girl with curly hair standing next to her looked at me. "Julianna."

The third girl, who had dark brown hair and a golden tan, didn't tell me her name at all.

Okay, I thought. *Let's get this over with!*

But that wasn't going to be as easy as we thought. We milled outside for at least twenty minutes, and nobody told us what to do. Then I realized I didn't see a photographer.

I walked over to the woman with the clipboard who had greeted me and overheard her talking to a guy in a yellow T-shirt with a *YL* logo on it and the word "youthleisure" underneath it in script.

"I'm sorry, Marcus is always late," she was saying. "But you wanted the best, and he's the best!"

"Fine, but I'm not paying everyone to wait for him," the guy responded.

"Actually, you are," the woman told him. "It's in your contract."

The man scowled and walked away. I headed over to Mom.

"I think the photographer's late," I told her. "Do you think we'll still make it to the game?" I thought of Jessi and her warnings.

She looked at her phone. "We still have hours until the game starts. I think we'll be fine," she said. Then she looked me up and down. "Very nice, Devin. I like this outfit."

"Me too," Maisie said. "You look pretty."

"Thanks," I said. I knew I would be on Maisie's good side for a little while, since I'd let her come to the shoot. At least I had that going for me.

So we waited for the photographer. And we waited . . . and waited some more.

"I am sooooo bored," Maisie moaned.

"Me too," I agreed.

"Can't we just leave?" Maisie asked.

"I don't think that would be professional," I replied.

Mom frowned. "I don't think this photographer is being very professional," she said.

The photographer, a blond guy wearing sunglasses, finally showed up around ten o'clock.

Delia stormed up to him. "Marcus, seriously?"

He shrugged. "Traffic, Delia," he said with a yawn. "Not my fault."

Delia rolled her eyes. "The models are ready for you."

Marcus started ordering around some people whom I guessed were assistants, and they set up two cameras in front of this big weeping willow tree. Then Delia snapped at us to all stand by the tree.

Marcus didn't even ask us our names.

"Girl in blue! Lean against the tree! Girl in pink, stand next to her!"

I obeyed and stood next to Aubrey.

"Other side!" Marcus barked, and I quickly moved to what I thought was the right position. Then he got the other models to pose too.

But then he kept making us move around. "Pink, switch with green! No, no, no. Move closer. Not that close."

This must have gone on for half an hour, at least, before he started taking any photos.

"Smile!" he yelled.

We all smiled. But I sure didn't feel like it. I don't think any of the other girls did either. Marcus couldn't even bother to learn our names. I felt like a prop, not a person. It made me think about how the photographer was like a coach. They could get the best out of you by being nice, like Coach Flores. They could even be super strict, like Coach Darby, and you could still learn a lot. But even though Coach Darby was tough, she called us all by name. At least when you joined a team, you got to know your coach, and they got to know you. But so far with modeling, I've worked with a new photographer every time, and clearly they were all very different.

Finally, after it seemed like we'd posed in every way possible, I thought we were finally done. I was eager to get changed and get to my game before I let my entire team down.

"Can we get changed yet?" Julianna asked.

"Not yet," Delia said. "Marcus might need more shots."

And of course, Marcus did want more shots. He wanted the tan girl who didn't tell me her name to put her hair in a ponytail. He wanted Aubrey and Julianna to switch hoodies. Then we took some *more* photos.

"Pink, show some teeth when you smile!" he told me.

And then, "No, Pink, smile with your eyes only and close your mouth!"

It was like nothing we did made him happy!

It was a quarter to twelve by the time he finished

the second round of shots. I anxiously waited on the sidelines with Mom as he looked over the footage he had taken.

"That's a wrap!" he called out, and I sighed with relief.

"Great," I told Mom. "We can still make it to the game on time."

Mom nodded. "Right. Just change into your uniform, and I'll take you right to the field."

Then it hit me. "Um, I forgot to bring my uniform with me." I'd gotten off on such a wrong foot that morning that I hadn't even thought of it.

"Devin!" Mom said, and then she sighed. "It's fine. We should still make it in time."

Of course, we weren't counting on Southern California freeway traffic. That's how I knew, by 11:55, that I wasn't going to make it to the game on time. According to Mom's phone, it was going to take an hour just to get to our house!

"This is terrible!" I groaned. "It's all because of that stupid Marcus!"

"Devin, you know we don't use that word," Mom said. "But yes, it certainly does seem to be his fault."

"I'm glad I didn't get discovered!" Maisie piped up from the backseat. "Being a model is so boring! And that guy was mean!"

"He wasn't mean, exactly," I said, thinking about it. "He just wasn't very friendly."

"He didn't even bother to learn your names," Mom said.

"That was very demeaning. And he didn't respect your time."

"He would have been happier with a bunch of card-board cutouts he could have moved around the set!" I joked, but mom was right. The whole experience was kind of demeaning.

"You'd better text Coach Flores and tell her you'll be late," Mom said.

I was dreading doing that, but I knew I had to. She texted me back.

Okay. Do your best to get here, Devin! We're counting on you!

I will, I promised.

It was almost one when we pulled into our driveway. I got dressed in record time. Knowing I had missed the sock swap, I pulled on two different socks. I didn't need any more bad luck than I'd already had!

When we got to the field, the game was in full swing. The scoreboard read KENTVILLE-2, HARRISON-2. The Bees, in their yellow uniforms with black stripes, really did look like bees zipping around the field.

I jogged up to Coach Flores.

"So sorry, Coach," I told her.

"I'll put you in for the second half," she said. "We're almost there."

I nodded and took my place on the bench, grateful that Coach Flores wasn't as strict as some other coaches. In the winter league, Coach Darby had a no-tolerance policy for lateness. If you were late, you didn't play.

The halftime whistle blew, and Jessi ran off the field and right to me.

"Let me guess," she said. "Your modeling thing went too long?"

I nodded. "You were right."

I worried she'd be mad, but then she grinned. "I love being right. But I hate that we're tied. We need you. And also, you missed Frida acting like a weird beekeeper."

She nodded toward Frida, who ran past a group of the Bees on the field, saying, "You shall not sting me! I am your master!"

I laughed. "Oh boy."

"But seriously, we need to beat these Bees," she said. "Is Coach letting you play the second half?"

I nodded. "Thankfully."

Jessi smiled. "Then let's kick some bee butt!"

Jessi and I high-fived, and a few minutes later, I was out on the grass, playing forward. As I ran down the field, my heart pumping, I found that my concentration was scattered.

I closed my eyes briefly and took a few deep breaths, just like I had learned in my smiling tutorial. I opened my eyes and smiled, feeling more focused. I wasn't thinking about anything except getting the ball in the net. Within the first five minutes, I intercepted a pass from one Bee to another and then kicked it to Hailey, who was in goal position. She scored, breaking the tie we had and making the game 3–2.

"Yes!" I cheered.

After being treated like a prop all morning, with a photographer who didn't even bother to learn my name, I felt in my element on the soccer field. The thought of letting my team down because I had been late inspired me to do my best and push aside my guilt. Being part of a team, hearing us call out one another's names, patting one another on the back when we had a good play, and just the overall camaraderie made me feel like this was where I belonged. Not to mention Coach Flores calling words of encouragement from the sidelines and giving us her all. The Kicks were not only my team; they were also my family, and I wasn't about to disappoint them.

The rest of the game went by in a whirlwind, and if I had been angry or frustrated that morning, I forgot all about it. I became laser-focused. I needed my soccer-ball brain now more than ever. I intercepted the ball four more times and managed to score two goals. Jessi and Grace both scored too, and we won handily in the end, 7–3.

"Go, Kicks!" the team cheered after we shook hands with the Bees.

"We should go out for pizza," Jessi said. She turned to me. "Unless you've got another modeling gig and you need to ditch us."

I knew she was teasing, so I joked back. "I don't know. Let me call my agent and find out."

Jessi groaned. "Seriously?"

"*Not* seriously," I said. "I like modeling, but today was

a lot different and just not as fun as soccer. Plus, I hated letting the team down, even though we still won."

"Yeah, I was bummed you missed the first half today," Jessi reminded me.

"I know," I said. "That will never happen again. I just won't book a shoot on the day of a game."

"Mmm-hmm," Jessi said in a voice that meant she didn't really believe me. I didn't like that feeling at all.

Then Emma, Frida, and Zoe ran up to us. Emma dragged me by the arm. "Come on! Pizza! My mom's driving."

I noticed she wasn't wearing her glasses. "Are you wearing contacts now?"

She nodded. "They're not as bad as I thought. And today I didn't hit anybody in the head with the ball by mistake!"

"Awesome," I said. "So I guess 'seeing things in a new way' is working out for you."

"I guess you could say that." She grinned.

Zoe rolled her eyes. "Not that app stuff again."

"Don't be so negative, Zoe," Frida said. "I bet you are still going to make a new friend."

"I highly doubt it," Zoe said.

"Can we please get in Mrs. Kim's van?" Jessi asked. "I need to make friends with a slice of pepperoni pizza!"

"Me too," I agreed. "But I'm thinking I might be even better friends with a chicken ranch slice."

We climbed into Mrs. Kim's van. It's one of those huge vehicles with three rows of seats. Jessi and I climbed into the very backseat, giggling as our arms and legs got tangled.

"I bet models don't go out for pizza after a photo shoot," Jessi said.

"You're right. We don't," I agreed, and that got me thinking. Modeling might be competitive, but so far, it was nothing like playing soccer. Every shoot was with different people. And while many of them were friendly, not all of them were. There is nothing like bonding with your teammates. After all, when I first moved to California, I didn't have a single friend. But thanks to the Kicks, I had a whole carful of them! I realized that what I liked best about modeling was what I liked best about playing soccer: when I could be active, contribute to ideas that helped the team (or the shoot), and do a good job. Except with soccer, I didn't have to force it. Even though I had to work hard, train, and practice for soccer, it all seemed to come more naturally to me. I had a lot to think about before I got back in front of a camera.

CHAPTER TWELVE

"Welcome to the South County Animal Shelter. I'm Lynn. Thanks for volunteering today!"

All of the Kicks, along with Coach Flores, were standing outside the animal shelter building on Sunday morning. Lynn, the volunteer coordinator, was a tall woman with wavy blond hair. She wore a blue T-shirt that read SOUTH COUNTY ANIMAL SHELTER, with a picture of a dog and a cat inside a heart. In the background, we could hear dogs yipping, barking, and howling.

"All of the animals here in the shelter are waiting to find their forever homes," Lynn said. "And while they're waiting, they need the same kind of attention and care that every animal needs. They need exercise and they need to interact with other people. That's where you all come in. Since you're athletes, you can give our dogs a good workout!"

"That's right! Go, Kicks!" Jessi called out, and we all started clapping.

"Great! Love the enthusiasm," Lynn said. "I'll need a dozen volunteers to walk the dogs. The rest of you can help out in the kitten room."

Zoe's hand shot up. "Kittens, please!"

"Me too!" Frida chimed in.

"I think I'd like to walk a dog," said Emma.

I looked at Jessi. We'd never had a pet because Dad has bad allergies to a lot of stuff, so I didn't have strong feelings about cats or dogs either way. They both seemed cute to me.

"I'm a dog person," Jessi said.

I nodded. "Cool. I feel like a walk, anyway."

Everybody began talking excitedly at once.

"Dog walkers, follow me, please!" Lynn called out over our voices. "Kitten people, please go see Holly over there."

I waved to Zoe and Frida, and then Emma, Jessi, and I followed Lynn, along with Coach Flores and the other girls on the team who wanted to walk dogs. We walked across the grounds of the shelter, a sprawling complex of three one-story concrete buildings. Lynn led us into the one where the sound of dogs barking was coming from.

"The dogs get very excited when they get visitors," she told us. "It might be hard to hear me, so stick close!"

She opened the door and we followed her inside. The sound of the dogs became almost deafening as soon as they saw us. Each one was in its own small pen with wire fencing on the doors. The room led out to a small fenced-in outdoor run.

Lynn stopped in front of one of the doors, where a big dog with silvery-gray fur was barking excitedly. Lynn picked up a leash hanging outside the door and stepped inside the pen. Then she clipped the leash to the dog's collar.

She came back out, leading the dog, and handed him to Coach Flores.

"Coach Flores, you can take Billy," she said. "Please take him outside and wait, and I'll send the rest of the girls and dogs out. Then you can all walk together."

"Got it!" Coach said, and she and Billy jogged outside.

In the next pen sat a little black-and-white dog, not barking, but looking at us with hopeful eyes. My heart melted.

"This is Angel. She's a Boston terrier," Lynn told us. She leashed Angel and then handed her over to Emma.

"You are an angel, aren't you?" Emma asked the pup. "Come on, girl."

Emma and Angel headed outside as Lynn put the leash on the next dog, a huge, shaggy mutt with floppy ears.

"You can take Sam," she told Jessi, handing her the leash.

"Cool name, Sam," Jessi said. "Let's go!"

Inside the next pen, a little white fluffy dog was jumping up and down and yipping.

"How you doing, Honey?" Lynn asked as she put the leash on the dog. "It's time for a walk!"

The little dog spun around in circles, twisting up her leash. I laughed.

"Why don't you take Honey?" Lynn asked, and I took the leash. The little dog started to run down the hallway at rocket speed, and I raced with her. I was worried at first that I'd lose her, but my legs were a lot longer than hers, so it was easy to keep pace.

I caught up to Emma and Jessi outside, and we waited for the other dog walkers to join us. Emma's dog, Angel, was sniffing the ground and making a funny snorting noise, and Emma was cracking up.

"She's like a little potbellied pig!" Emma said. "Adorable!"

Sam was straining on the leash, eager to get walking. Jessi patted him on the head. "Steady now, Sam. We'll be going soon." He nuzzled her hand and calmed down.

Honey, though, could not be still. She hopped, she twirled, and she ran circles around my legs so I kept getting tangled in the leash. "Honey, I wish I had your energy on the soccer field!" I told her.

After just a few minutes, we were all gathered outside. Lynn handed each of us two small plastic bags.

"You'll be walking the dogs down that path," she said, pointing to a tree-lined path that led away from the shelter. "Let's walk for at least twenty minutes. Make sure you clean up after the dogs; there's a garbage can back here where you can put the bags. And while these dogs are friendly, please don't let them stop and interact with any other dogs. This is about exercising, not socializing."

"All right, let's go!" Coach Flores said.

Sam charged ahead, dragging Jessi behind him.

"Jessi, this isn't a race!" Coach called out.

"Tell that to Sam!" Jessi answered.

Honey continued to do a happy dance, jumping and circling as we walked. Emma and Angel walked beside us. Honey tried to get Angel's attention, but the little Boston terrier kept her nose to the ground, smelling everything in her path.

"These dogs are so cute!" Emma said. "I can't believe they ended up in a shelter."

Coach overheard us. "There are many reasons why animals end up in shelters. Sometimes, their owners simply can't take care of them anymore. But most times, people get dogs that aren't suited for them and think they've made a mistake. Instead of figuring out how to work with the dog, or get the dog trained, they surrender them."

I looked down at cute little Honey, and thinking of her being surrendered almost broke my heart.

"I guess a dog like Honey would need a lot of attention," I said.

"Exactly," Coach said. "And she probably wouldn't be happy staying home alone all day."

"Devin, your mom works from home during the day," Emma said. "*You* could take Honey!"

I shook my head. "My dad is allergic to dogs. And a

bunch of other stuff." I frowned. "You know, I never really thought about having a dog before. But now that I've met these dogs, I wish I could have one!"

"You could always keep volunteering at the shelter," Coach Flores suggested. "I know they always need help here."

"Maybe I could," I said, but then I frowned. Since I'd started modeling, I hadn't had much time for anything else except soccer and homework. I wasn't sure how I'd fit volunteering into that schedule. And I'd hate to let the shelter down if a shoot ran long like the last one.

We took the dogs for a nice long walk and then returned to the shelter. I noticed Zoe's mom, Mrs. Quinlan, getting out of her car in the parking lot.

That's weird, I thought, because my mom was supposed to be the one picking us up. But before I could think about it further, a woman and a man rushed up to me. The woman had a bright pink streak in her hair and a shirt with a rainbow on it, and the man's T-shirt read IT TAKES A BIG MAN TO WALK A SMALL DOG.

"There she is! There's Honey!" the woman cried.

Honey started yipping like crazy when she saw them. The woman knelt down and started petting Honey. "Do you remember us?" she asked the dog.

"You know Honey?" I asked.

"We met her yesterday," the woman said. She stood up and held out her hand. "I'm Katie, and this is my husband, Gary. We came to see Honey yesterday and fell in love with her. We put in our adoption application and just got the call that she's ours."

"Wow, really?" I said. They both seemed really nice. "That's awesome."

"Our dog died a few months ago," Gary said. "We miss her a lot. And Honey reminds us of her."

"So much energy!" Katie said. She knelt down again. "You're going to like it at our house, Honey. We've got a nice fenced-in yard. Plenty of room to run and play."

Lynn walked up and took the leash from my hand. "Thanks for walking her," she told me. Then she looked at Honey. "I'm going to miss you, girl!"

She gave the leash to Katie, and she and Gary took Honey over to the shelter's main office. I was so glad she'd be getting a new home today. That's when I noticed that Zoe was outside with her mom—and cradling a tiny black kitten.

Curious, I jogged over to Zoe while the other girls brought the dogs back inside.

"Hi, Mrs. Quinlan," I said to Zoe's mom.

"Hi, Devin," she replied.

"Um, I thought my mom was picking us up?" I asked.

"She still is," Mrs. Quinlan replied. "I'm only here because Zoe texted me a picture of this little cutie." She patted the little black kitten on its head.

"Isn't she precious?" Zoe asked. "Listen—she's purring!"

"She's awfully cute," I agreed.

Zoe looked at her mom. "What do you think? Can we adopt her?" she asked, her blue eyes wide.

"I wouldn't have come down here if I wasn't thinking about it," her mom replied. "Does she have all of her shots?"

Zoe nodded. "She's healthy. She just needs to be spayed."

"And does she get along with other cats?" her mom asked. "Butterball is a sweetheart, but she's used to being the only cat in the house."

"They said she's very sweet with all of the other kittens," Zoe said. "Please, Mom? Butterball is basically Jayne's cat, anyway. I'll take care of little Coco all by myself. I promise."

Mrs. Quinlan nodded. "Let's go inside and fill out the application."

That's when Frida walked up. She looked at Mrs. Quinlan, and then at Zoe holding the cat. She let out a gasp and ran up to them.

"Are you adopting that kitten?" she asked.

"We're going to apply," Zoe answered, and then her eyes narrowed suspiciously. "No. Don't you dare say it."

"But I have to say it! Your fortune came true! You *have* made a new friend!" Frida said.

"I warned you not to say it," Zoe said, shaking her head.

"What is this about?" Zoe's mom asked.

"Nothing," Zoe said quickly. "Let's go fill out the forms."

"Come on, Devin," Frida said to me after they'd gone inside. "You have to admit that this is more than a coincidence."

"Hmmm," I said slowly. "Is a cat the same as a friend?"

"Of course it is!" Frida replied. "Sometimes animals can be even better friends than people." Then she counted silently on her fingers. "That's four fortunes that have come true, Devin. You're the last one! I bet soon, you're going to hear about a big trip."

I thought about the trip I *wanted* to take to Connecticut. But Mom hadn't said anything about it in days, and I'd stopped asking her so that "maybe" didn't become "no."

"I don't know about that, Frida," I said.

She stared at me, and then she wiggled her fingers in a spooky way. "Flash Fortune never lies, Devin," she said. "You'll see!"

CHAPTER THIRTEEN

"Ice cream! Ice cream! Can we get ice cream?"

Maisie was bouncing up and down and pulling on my mother's hand. After I'd come home from helping at the animal shelter, Dad had suggested that we go to the beach. It was a beautiful afternoon, not too hot, and a nice breeze was blowing.

When we lived in Connecticut, going to the beach was a big deal. We had to pack the car with all our gear and drive for an hour and a half to get there, and sit in traffic. Now that we lived in California, we could walk to the beach if we wanted to.

Since it was a nice day, we decided to do just that. We set up a blanket and an umbrella, and Mom sprayed sunscreen on both me and Maisie. Just after that, the ice cream guy came by, pushing his cart on the sand.

"Now, Maisie," Mom said. "We're going to eat dinner tonight at Captain Jack's Seafood Shack. You don't want to spoil your appetite."

"Captain Jack's?" Maisie asked. "With the free pirate hats?"

"That's right," Mom said.

"Yay!" Maisie cheered. Then she ran off toward the water, forgetting the ice cream entirely.

"Keep an eye on your sister, please," Mom said, settling into her beach chair and opening up a book.

"Sure," I said. I joined Maisie, shivering at first as the cold water hit my legs.

Maisie ran up to me. "Let's go deeper."

I held her hand and we walked forward. She giggled as a wave crashed into us.

"Hold your nose!" I told her, and together we dove under the next wave that hit us.

We swam for a while and then walked back onshore. A girl streaked by us, kicking a beach ball with her bare foot. She passed it to a group of girls who were playing what looked like a pickup game in the sand.

"Beach soccer!" Maisie yelled. She ran toward the girls, and I chased after her.

It turns out the girls were playing with a beach ball and beach chairs that marked out the goal space. They were happy to let Maisie and me join them. We must have played with them for an hour, laughing as we kicked the ball up and down the beach.

When we got back to our umbrella, Mom was shaking her head.

"You girls really love soccer," she said. "Devin, you just had a game yesterday, and you've got practice tomorrow, and here you are playing it again on your day off!"

"I do love soccer," I admitted. It had been so fun, I'd never even hesitated or thought I should take a break.

Mom held up the sunscreen can. "More sunscreen," she said. "If you want to swim some more, do it now. We're going to Captain Jack's in an hour."

Maisie couldn't stop talking as we walked all the way to the restaurant a little later. "I'm going to get a free pirate hat," she said. "And order the shrimp. And you need to take my picture with the talking parrot. And then I'm going to ask the waitress for an extra piece of pirate bread, because they only ever give you one, and it's soooo delicious. . . ."

When we got to Captain Jack's, a plaster pirate statue greeted us at the doorway. A red robotic parrot was perched on his shoulder. The parrot's head swiveled from side to side when we approached.

"All aboard for delicious food!" The parrot squawked.

Maisie ran up to the parrot. "Take my picture!" she demanded.

Mom snapped a picture with her phone. "Okay, but I want this to be a phone-free dinner. I don't want to be one of those families who stare at their screens instead of at one another."

The restaurant was packed, and we had to wait for our table. Maisie demanded her free cardboard pirate hat while we were waiting, and she put it on right away. I got out my phone since we weren't seated yet and took a photo of the pirate ship on the hostess stand and texted it to Frida.

This is the closest I'll get to a trip! I told her.

Unbeliever! she texted back with a dozen pirate emojis.

Fifteen minutes later, the hostess told us our table was ready. As we were sitting down, Mom's phone pinged.

"Let me just check this," Mom said.

"I thought you said no phones!" Maisie protested.

"I'll put it away right after this," Mom promised. She read the screen. "Devin, it's Ashanta. She's got a job for you on Wednesday."

"Wednesday?" I asked. "But I have practice."

"I know," Mom said. "It's up to you, Devin."

The next words came out of my mouth before I even thought about saying them. "I don't think I want to model anymore," I said, and as soon as I did, I felt relieved.

"Are you sure, Devin?" Mom asked, but she looked relieved too.

I nodded. "I am really glad I tried modeling. I learned a lot, and it definitely got me out of my comfort zone. I was really surprised to learn that there are a lot of similarities between soccer and modeling. I wasn't expecting that!" I laughed. "But where I feel most important, and most valuable, is on the soccer field. I can't imagine not being part of a soccer team, and I also can't imagine being part of a soccer team and not being able to give myself one-hundred-percent to it. Something has to come first, and for me, that something is definitely soccer."

I took a deep breath. "I'm sorry I won't be saving money for college. Maybe I'll try to get soccer scholarships. Maybe I'll try to go pro. And that will take a lot of work."

"We'll support you, Devin," Dad said. "I think you're making a good decision as long as soccer is what you really love."

"So do I," Mom agreed.

"Me too!" Maisie said. "Modeling is sooooo boring!"

"I'll let Ashanta know," Mom said. "And then I'll put away my phone."

"I've also been thinking that I'd like to volunteer at the animal shelter," I said. "Modeling was so unpredictable, it left no time for anything else but soccer and school."

My mom and dad exchanged nervous glances.

"That's very kind of you, Devin," Mom said slowly. "But we need to make it clear that you can't bring any animals home. Your dad's allergies would make that impossible."

"Don't worry, I know," I told them. "Being at the shelter with the dogs is the next best thing to having a pet. I promise I won't bring any home."

Maisie pouted. "Awwww, come on! I want a dog! Don't they make medicine for allergies? I saw a commercial the other day, and this guy was playing with a puppy and he was sneezing, but then he took this pill and he was fine. And the puppy was jumping all over him and licking his face! It was sooooo cute!"

Mom sighed. "Maisie, we've talked about this. Dad's allergies are more severe than that."

I was in such a good mood, now that I didn't feel torn between soccer and modeling, that it made me feel very generous with Maisie. "Maybe you can come with me and help out at the shelter too? That way you can get your puppy time in."

"Yay!" Maisie cheered.

"Hey, maybe we could even take pictures of the dogs to give them really nice photos for their adoption website? I think I might have learned a thing or two on the photo shoots!" I said.

Mom beamed. "I think that's a great idea, Devin."

Just then, Dad's phone pinged. He glanced at his screen. This dinner was becoming nothing but phones.

"It's the office," he said. "Just one sec."

He scrolled through his screen. Then he looked at my mom. "Looks like they definitely want me in Connecticut for that sales presentation," he said. "Should we tell her?"

"Tell me what?" Maisie and I both asked.

Dad looked at me. "Devin, I'll be going to Connecticut for a few days for work. And those days happen to be at the same time as your friend Charlotte's party. So if you don't mind using some of your modeling money . . ."

I squealed. "You mean I can go?"

"Yes, you can go," Mom said.

Maisie frowned and folded her arms across her chest. "It's not fair! Devin gets to go on a plane and I don't!"

"How about I give you my piece of pirate bread?" I offered.

"That's a start," Maisie said.

I held up my phone. "Mom, can I text Kara? Please?"

Mom nodded. "Fine. But then all phones away! I mean it!"

I quickly texted. **Good news! I can go to Charlotte's party!**

Kara replied with a string of emojis. 😊 🎉 🎈 🎆

I grinned—and then I realized I had one more text to send. I quickly sent it before Mom could object. This one went to Frida.

I'm a believer, I typed, and then I quickly stashed my phone away before the barrage of replies came from her. I'd tell her everything later.

The server came to our table.

"May I take your order?" she asked.

"I will please have the Junior Pirate Shrimp Platter," Maisie said. Then she pointed to me. "And *she* is giving me her pirate bread."

I didn't mind. I was so happy and excited that I could barely eat.

I had a goal I was ready to really work for, and I was going back to Connecticut to see my friends. I couldn't wait!

TURN THE PAGE FOR A SNEAK PEEK AT
HOMECOMING

THE KICKS
HOMECOMING

16

Charlotte

★ BY WORLD CUP CHAMPION AND OLYMPIC GOLD MEDALIST ★
ALEX MORGAN

CHAPTER ONE

Adrenaline pumped through my body as I raced down the field. One of the Marlins was dribbling at rocket speed toward the Kicks goal, and none of our defending midfielders could catch up to her. With her hands on her knees in front of the goal, Emma waited for the ball, eyes alert. The score was tied, 17–17, and the clock was running down.

Wham! The Marlin kicked the ball hard. Emma lunged for it, and it bounced off her gloved hands, careening back onto the field. The same player got control of it again.

My friend Frida, a Kicks defender, charged up to her. Frida was an actor who pretended to be different characters to gain courage on the soccer field. Today she was a pirate.

"Aaargh. We shall give no quarter to thieves who try to steal our pirate gold!" she yelled.

Frida's strange cry startled the Marlin, who stumbled just enough for Frida to kick the ball away from her. It went flying and landed between another Marlin and Zoe, who got to it first, which was not a surprise because she had some of the fastest moves I've ever seen. She dribbled toward the Marlins' goal, with the player who missed out on the ball at her heels.

I changed direction to get clear in case Zoe wanted to pass. She kicked it right to me just as the player behind her caught up to her.

I got control of the ball and dribbled into Marlin territory. In twenty feet I'd be close enough to shoot . . .

I saw a turquoise-and-white blur out of the corner of my left eye. One of the Marlins was coming at me fast. I turned and saw another defender charging toward me from the front.

"Devin! Over here!"

Jessi called to me from my right. I turned to face her and saw that she was clear.

Wham! I sent the ball skidding across the grass. Jessi stopped it and zoomed toward the goal. I could hear our fans screaming in the stands.

"Go, Jessi!"

"Go, Kicks!"

Jessi got within range and sent the ball soaring. I stopped, watching it fly through the air. The Marlins goalie jumped up to block it, but she fell short. It grazed the top of her fingers and slammed into the net.

The ref blew her whistle. *Game over!*

"The Kicks win!" somebody shouted.

I ran to Jessi and slapped her on the back. "You were awesome!"

She grinned at me. "*We* were awesome, you mean," she said. "Thanks for setting me up."

"No problem," I said.

We ran to line up with the rest of our teammates, to slap hands with the Marlins. I knew how much it hurt to lose—especially when a game was that close—and I could see the disappointment on their faces.

After I slapped the last palm, I jogged back to the sideline where the Kicks were gathering. When everyone arrived, we huddled in a circle, jumping up and down with excitement.

"Great game, everybody!" congratulated Grace, an eighth grader and my co-captain.

Coach Flores approached us, and we broke up the circle.

"Good work, girls!" she said. "This means we've made the playoffs!"

We began yelling and cheering.

"You all certainly earned it," Coach continued as we quieted down. "The first playoff game is in two weeks, so our practice schedule is going to change a bit. Our weekday practices will continue. But there's a break next weekend, with no regular games, so we'll practice at ten a.m. that Saturday."

Megan, another eighth grader, raised her hand. "Do we know who we're playing in the first game?"

Coach shook her head. "No, but we'll know when all of

today's games are finished. I'll send out a group text when I get the word."

"This is great news," said Grace. "Let's go to Pizza Kitchen to celebrate!"

Everybody started packing up their water bottles and duffel bags. Jessi, Emma, Zoe, Frida, and I gravitated toward one another as we got ready to go. We all looked like kind of a mess, except for Zoe, who always managed to look neat and whose short, blond hair kept her head cool when she played. Jessi's long braids helped with the heat, too, but like me, her jersey was soaked with sweat. Frida's curly auburn hair was falling out of the high bun she'd had it in, and Emma's arms and legs were streaked with dirt from her diving after the ball.

"That game was intense, and I'm starving!" Jessi said. "I'm going to eat a whole pizza by myself."

"I'm pretty hungry too," Zoe said. "Want to split a veggie pizza with me when we get there, Devin?"

"I can't go, remember?" I said. "I've got to go get my dress for Charlotte's party."

"Aw, come on. That's, like, a week away," Jessi said. "We made the playoffs! You have to celebrate with us!"

"I know, but Sabine is helping me pick it out, and this is the only time she's free," I explained.

"You know, I should be insulted that you didn't ask *me*," Zoe said. "But Sabine is flawless, so I understand."

"Oh, no!" I said. "I told Sabine I was going to a sweet sixteen party, so she offered to take me shopping, but I should've totally thought to ask you. I'm sorry."

"Don't worry about it," Zoe replied. "Just send us a picture so we can see how gorgeous you look, okay?"

"I promise," I said, and I glanced at Jessi. By her frowny face I knew she was upset that I wasn't going to celebrate our big win.

I hugged her.

"Go get your pizza. I'll be there in spirit," I told her.

"I'll make sure to eat an extra slice for you," Jessi promised, and I knew that everything was good between us.

I headed back home with Mom, Dad, and Maisie, who had come to cheer me on at the game because they're awesome. I showered and changed into shorts and a T-shirt when I got home, a fitting outfit for an 80-degree day. It was that warm even though it was still spring. That wasn't unusual for Southern California, but it was my first spring living here. Almost a year before, my family had moved here from Connecticut, and less than a week from now I was heading back for a few days.

My best friend in Connecticut was Kara. She and I talked almost every day, and I still missed her. I missed seeing her at school and playing on the same soccer team. It helped that I'd made some new best friends here in California, but I wished Kara could be part of my life here too.

When Kara and I were in third grade, an older girl named Charlotte was our soccer mentor. Now Charlotte was turning sixteen and she had invited both me and Kara to come to her sweet sixteen party. I had thought that I wouldn't be able to go, but then Dad had found out he had to go back to Connecticut for a meeting, and he'd said he'd bring me with him.

I was kind of excited to be going back to Connecticut, and totally psyched for Charlotte's party. I was less excited when Kara told me I needed to find a semiformal dress for it, though, because fashion was not my thing. That was when Sabine had offered to help.

Sabine and I had met on a modeling job. For a hot second I'd done some photo shoots for sports fashions, until I'd decided that modeling wasn't for me.

The best thing about it was meeting Sabine. She modeled too, but she went to another school, so I never would have met her if I hadn't done those gigs.

When I was ready, Mom drove me to the mall to meet Sabine.

"Text me when you find a dress you like, and I'll come check it out," Mom told me as we walked to the fountain in the center of the mall. "I need to find a new yoga mat."

Sabine was waiting for us by the fountain.

"Devin!" she called out, and I swear her perfect white teeth gleamed when she smiled at me. Zoe was right—Sabine was flawless, without a hair out of place or a pimple on her smooth, brown skin. Thanks to a daily combination of sweat and sunscreen, three bright red pimples had popped up on my pale white chin just that morning.

"Hey, Sabine," I said. "Thanks for helping me find a dress!"

"Yes, thanks," my mom said. "Please guide Devin toward

something youthful and tasteful? And not too short?"

"Mom!" I said.

"Don't worry, Mrs. Burke," Sabine said. "I actually have the perfect dress picked out already. I think you'll like it."

"Terrific! Devin will text me once you've figured it out," Mom said, and then she waved and took off.

"Congrats on winning your game today," Sabine said.

"Thanks—wait. How did you know?" I asked.

"Zoe texted me," she replied.

"Oh, right," I said. After I'd told Zoe about Sabine, they'd connected on social media. I knew they had a lot in common, and I'd had a hunch that they could be friends. It sounded like they'd clicked pretty fast—so I'd been right!

"How was your photo shoot yesterday?" I asked.

Sabine rolled her eyes. "It went on for *hours*," she said. "The client was there, and she kept telling the photographer what I should do, and she kept changing her mind. 'Smile. Don't smile! Smile. Don't smile!'" Sabine shook her head. "I think I pulled a mouth muscle."

I laughed. "I'm glad I decided to stick to soccer," I told her.

"I get it. But, Devin, you were *good*," she said. "Anyway, you need to model one more time, in this dress I picked out. Come on."

She took my hand, and I followed her through the packed mall. We ended up at a big shop called Belle of the Ball, with lots of fancy dresses in the window. My eyes widened.

"These look like runway gowns," I said. "Are you sure I'm supposed to wear something like this?"

"This shop has semiformal dresses too, and I found one that will work perfectly. Trust me," Sabine said.

She led me through the shop to a rack of dresses and pulled out a light blue one with little sparkly stones scattered across it that reminded me of stars.

"The blue goes with your eyes," she said. "Try it on!"

I obeyed and tried on the dress in the changing room. It was sleeveless, with a straight neckline and a skirt that went out at the waist. I looked at myself in the mirror. The skirt hit right at my knee—not too short, just like Mom had asked for. Even with my pimples, and my skinned knee from practice, I thought I looked beautiful.

I swung my arms, and then I did a twirl. The dress was comfortable, too! It was amazing!

"Come on, Devin!" Sabine urged from outside the curtain.

I stepped out of the changing booth, and Sabine smiled widely. "It's spectacular! You look gorgeous!"

"I love it," I admitted. "In fact, I don't think I've ever looked this good in anything. You are a genius!"

"When I was scoping out the dresses, I just knew this was the one," she said.

I went back into the booth, took out my phone, and gave it to her. "Can you take my picture, please?"

"Sure," she said. She held up the phone. "Let's see some model poses, Devin. Smile! Don't smile! Now smile!"

I stuck my tongue out at her. "Very funny," I said. I took the phone from her. "But thank you."

I texted Mom the picture and the name of the store, and by the time I had changed back into my shorts and shirt, she was at the register, waiting for us.

"I love it!" she said. "Thank you so much, Sabine."

"You're welcome," Sabine replied. "I had a good time."

Mom paid for the dress and then took me and Sabine to the salad place for a late lunch. Then we dropped Sabine off at her house on our way home.

I walked into our house, clutching the bag with my dress in it. Weird, I know, but it was the first time I'd ever been in love with an item of clothing.

Maisie ran up to me. "Let me see it! Let me see it!"

I set the bag down on the coffee table and carefully pulled out the dress. Maisie's eyes went wide.

"It's a fairy princess dress!" she exclaimed. She turned to Mom. "How come Devin gets a fairy princess dress and I don't?"

"When you have a special event to go to, I will get you a fairy princess dress," Mom promised.

Maisie frowned. "How come Devin gets to go to a special event and I don't?"

Mom sighed. "Maisie, we've been over this."

I put the dress back into the bag and ran up the stairs, two at a time.

"Thanks, Mom! I'm going to show Kara!" I called behind me.

I ran into my room and closed the door. First I texted Kara the picture of me in the dress. Then I turned on my laptop and called her on video chat.

After a few beeps her face appeared on the screen.

"That dress is amazing!" she said. "Devin, I'm so excited!"

I held up the dress so she could see it again. "I know!" I said. "I'm excited too."

"My parents are getting me out of school early on Thursday so we can pick you and your dad up from the airport," Kara said, talking quickly. "And Friday I'm taking off from school and we're going to do something special, but it's a surprise. And we have practice before the party on Saturday night and you can come and watch. And—"

"Okay. Slow down. You're going to make my head explode!" I teased. "Trust me, I'm really excited to be going back ho—"

I stopped myself from saying "home." Connecticut used to be my home, but it wasn't anymore.

"We're going to have an awesome time," Kara promised. "Hey, I have to help make dinner. I'll see you in five days."

"Five days!" I replied, and then we ended the call. I was all happy and floaty.

The Kicks were going to the playoffs. I was going back to Connecticut to see Kara. And I was going to wear a beautiful dress and go to an awesome party.

I do feel like a fairy princess, I thought, and then I heard Jessi's voice in my head.

Really, Devin? What's next, are you going to grow wings?

I laughed, but then I got a little bit sad, thinking about how I would miss Jessi while I was visiting Kara.

But it was only for a few days.

CHAPTER TWO

"Only three more days of Devin," Emma said with a sigh. Then she popped a piece of cucumber sushi roll into her mouth. (Emma's mom packed her the most amazing lunches every day.)

My friends and I were eating in the cafeteria of Kentville Middle School. Today we'd scored a table outside in the beautiful Southern California sunshine.

"I'm not going away forever," I told her. "It's only for a few days. You won't even miss me."

"Of course we will!" Zoe said.

"We'll miss you at practice," Jessi added. "Especially since I found out that we're playing the Eagles in our first game. They're a strong team."

"Didn't we beat them?" I asked.

Jessi shook her head. "Nope. That was the day the eighth graders pretended to be sick and stayed home. Remember?"

The details of the game came flooding back to me. It

had been a hot day down at the Victorton field, and we'd had a hard time getting through the Eagles' defense. I started to sweat now, just thinking about it, but the heat wasn't why we had lost. We couldn't beat them because some of our strongest players had been missing.

"Well, that's not going to happen again," Emma pointed out. "The eighth graders only did that because they were mad at us. But everything's good now. We're all getting along."

"Still, we don't really know if we can beat them," Jessi said. "That's why we need to practice harder than ever. *All* of us." She looked at me.

"I'm only missing two practices," I said. "I'll be back in time for practice on Monday. That's plenty of time to get ready for the playoffs."

"Good," Jessi said. "Because I want to go all the way this time."

Everyone got quiet, remembering the playoffs at the end of the fall season. We had won the first two games, getting the league championship. But our bid for state had ended with a painful loss to the Brightville Bolts.

"This is way different from the fall season," I pointed out. "Going into the playoffs, we weren't playing as a team. Then Coach Flores's dad got sick, and Coach Valentine replaced her."

Frida shuddered. "I still have nightmares. He was so strict!"

"I think he was a good coach, but it threw us off our game," I said.

"Don't forget that the Kicks couldn't even win until you came along, Devin," Emma added.

I blushed. "You were always a good team. You just . . ."

"We needed a push in the right direction, and you gave it to us," Zoe finished for me. "Honestly, Devin, I don't know where we'd be if you hadn't moved here."

"Yeah. Sorry, Connecticut—we need Devin here!" Emma said.

From the critically acclaimed author of *Amina's Voice*
comes a slam dunk new chapter book series about a scrawny fourth
grader with big-time hoop dreams . . . if he can just get on the court.

Zayd Saleem, Chasing the Dream!

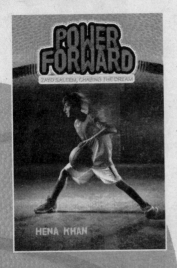

"Readers will
cheer for Zayd."

—*Kirkus Reviews*
on *Power Forward*

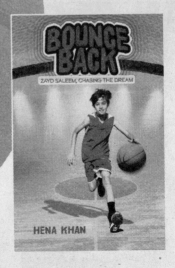

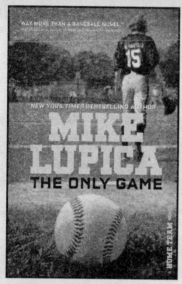